Editing: Joy Editing
Cover Model: Alfie Gordillo
Photographer: R + M Photography
Cover Design: Cover Me Darling

WICKED LITTLE SONGS
The Playlist

Available on Spotify here: http://bit.ly/WLWPlaylist

"Devil Inside Me"—Frank Carter & The Rattlesnakes

"Gasoline"—Halsey

"Don't Fear the Reaper"—Denmark + Winter

"Goner"—Twenty-One Pilots

"Closer"—Nine Inch Nails

"Creep"—Radiohead

"Pretty Monster"—Reckless Serenade

"Pain is a Gift"—Trade Wind

"Faces"—The Ratells

"Dark in My Imagination" – of Verona

"People Are Strange"—Goodbye Nova

"Devil Side" - Foxes

"Only the Lonely"—Iggy Pop

"I Really Want You to Hate Me"—Meg Myers

"Doomed"—Bring Me the Horizon

"Cry Little Sister"—Gerard McMann

"Possum Kingdom"—The Toadies

"Killing Time"—City & Colour

"My Name is Human"—Highly Suspect

"London Bridges"—Second Skin

"Take Her From You"—DEV

"Strange Love" - Halsey

"Down with the Sickness"—Disturbed

"Eyes on Fire"—Blue Foundation

"R&R"—The Classic Crime

"Big Bad Wolf"—In This Moment

"Limousine"—Brand New

"Paint It Black"- Ciara

"Words have no power to impress the mind without the exquisite horror of their reality." - *Edgar Allen Poe*

PROLOGUE
Edwin

"Devil Inside Me"—Frank Carter & The Rattlesnakes

It's the screaming that gets to me, tugging at the little bit of conscience I have left. Mind you, it's just a sliver. Screams die out quickly with a pair of panties and duct tape though. And I do just that to the whore strapped to my table—much like one you'd find in a prison's execution room. Perhaps you'd think the screams make me nervous. Maybe force me to abandon my sick plans. But you'd be wrong. My cabin in the hills of western North Carolina is completely isolated for ten miles in either direction. As the cold bite of fall makes its presence known, you're more likely to see a goddamn Sasquatch out here than you are another human being. But I'm in luck. I brought this one with me.

And that's not even getting to the true reason I don't worry—the six-inch-thick soundproof panels lining every inch of this shed. Several hundred feet behind my cabin is the kill shed I built with my own hands four years ago. Back before I made it big. Back when this writing thing was just a hobby.

Do you think any of those fucking readers paid attention to my writing before I started killing people? Before I started getting the murders in my own novels as *realistic* as possible? You bet your goddamn ass they didn't. They want the gore. They want the carnage. They want the mayhem. And goddamn it, I'm going to give it to them.

Eight *New York Times* best sellers so far in my short career. Million-dollar publishing and movie deals. More interview requests than my stomach can bear. At thirty-three years of age, I'd say I'm not doing too bad for myself. And of course, I turn down all those worthless interview requests. I'm not in this for the fame, nor have I ever been. I'm in this because people will *hear* me. They will *listen* to what I have to say. They will *feel* my words. To know that so many are reading and devouring my words, it's fucking orgasmic. I get hard just thinking about it.

But believe me, none of this, not a single fucking book sale, could've been accomplished without this bloodshed. Without the death I've created in this room. Without witnessing firsthand what a human being looks like truly suffering. What it looks like when the life drains from their face and the thousand-yard death stare follows. All of it makes its way into my novels. And all of it is gobbled up by my readers like it's fucking Thanksgiving dinner. You can blame me all you want for the deaths of these people, but it's the readers who deserve the blame. *They* want this. *They* yearn for it. And by God, I'm going to be the one to fucking give it to them.

It's not like I'm killing valuable, productive members of society here. These are fucking whores. Scum of the earth. How could someone sell their body for sex? What must have happened to a person in their life to lead them to that? And what easy pickings they make. If you trust a stranger and fuck a stranger, don't complain when things come back to bite you in the ass. That's just logic. If they can't smell it coming, they belong on my table.

I'd be lying if I said they were the only ones though. But the others had it coming too. I've never murdered an innocent without being provoked. So in the end, they weren't so innocent after all.

This one's an ugly little thing. Barely five feet tall, she was one of my easiest catches to date. The trunk of the rental (always a rental) housed her unconscious body (thank you, chloroform) all the way from Charlotte this time. I change the city each time—Asheville one week, Winton-Salem the next. The rental keeps their DNA out of my vehicle, and the change in cities, well, you're not that fucking stupid are you?

The hookers never hesitate to climb inside my car. I'm no fat old slob getting the only ass he can. I'm a good-looking guy. Still young enough to have a full head of brown hair, no grays, and I've been told by some that I'm Gavin

Rossdale's doppelgänger, which I'll take, but fuck that pussy. No, they never hesitate to trust me. And those who were cautious were only that way because they thought I was a pig. But by then, it was already too late. Once you're inside my car, not a soul on this planet can save you. Your life is mine to take.

Now I know you must be wondering... is he crazy? I can see how you could think that. But here's the thing: aren't we all a bit crazy in our own way? The fat fucking bastard ordering thirty tacos and a diet coke at Taco Bell— isn't he fucking crazy? The pill-popping soccer mom with her mouth around the pool boy's dick—isn't she a bit crazy too? Fuck what you think of me anyways. I'm a product of my environment through and through.

Dad hightailed the fuck out of there before I could even walk. Mommy dearest had a penchant for heroin and the temper of a convict. You think I had a choice? You think I asked to be her whipping boy for eighteen years? You think I fucking asked to wear a dress? Fuck no. I've found my path to success, and the headcount is worth its weight in gold.

But here I am, sitting with a fresh victim minutes or hours, or maybe even days, from death, and I'm staring mindlessly at a blank screen. The goddamn curser's flashing and flashing and flashing. The words are at the tip of my tongue but never quite make it to my fingertips. I want to slam the MacBook into her forehead until either the laptop or her skull breaks. I'd bet on the laptop, but I've learned, in this room, to never underestimate the strength of the most unorthodox murder weapons. I killed someone with a vacuum cleaner once. Just to see if I could do it.

I've had writer's block before—but never anything like this. This is a fucking nightmare beyond nightmares. The reviews for my last novel were abysmal (though it was still a best seller), and I knew then what I needed to do. I scoured hundreds of negative reviews, most calling for me to soften it up. They loved the murder and mayhem, but my voice, they said, had "become too dominant, too aggressive." They wanted me to become a woman. To pussify my writing.

That I cannot do. But what I can do is *find* a woman. The idea of co-writing makes me absolutely ill, but if I could find the right one... if I could find an innocent, easily manipulated little twat who will do my bidding then cease to exist, then I'll have my masterpiece. Then they'll have nothing to do but praise me for my work. They'll worship me. I would have the best of both worlds.

Perhaps I would imprison her for a while. Feed her just enough to keep her alive and have her assist on future releases. Got to keep the gravy train rolling! I've thought about it, even planned it a little. But they're just no fun when they're alive that long. The screaming, the begging, the fear in their eyes. That fear feeds me for a bit. But *days* of it? It's just a hassle. The longest I've kept one alive in my kill shed was a week. But that was because I was right at the climax of my story. I really needed to draw her out. To make her suffer until she just couldn't suffer anymore. As it turned out, a week was her max.

Now, the tough question to answer is how. How do I find her?

CHAPTER ONE
Miranda

"Gasoline"—Halsey

Dear Students,

Mr. Edwin Allen Mercer, NYT best-selling author, is accepting submissions for a possible co-author to collaborate with on his next novel. The submissions are open to all Creative Writing graduate programs in the United States. I believe this is a fantastic opportunity—a once-in-a-lifetime opportunity. To be considered, please write a five-thousand-word short story and submit the final draft to Mr. Mercer's assistant via email. The deadline is strict and set for February 2, 2016, all entries due in by midnight EST.

Best of luck,

Dr. Russell

Master's Program, Emory University

Email submissions to:

Wicked LITTLE WORDS

JanineBarnes@DarkInkPress.com

I push the announcement to the side of my desk and redirect my gaze to the computer screen. *Flash. Flash. Flash.* The blinking cursor taunts me—*Write something, Miranda. It's just words...* my fingers tap over the keyboard.

He slowly drags the blade over her skin, watching as her pale flesh tears open. Red blood seeps—Shit. Delete.

I watch the cursor wipe out that horrible sentence. Red blood? I roll my eyes. That's unoriginal.

Groaning, I slam my head on the keyboard. I've been sitting here for two hours and have a grand total of five hundred words. The deadline is midnight, and I need to write forty-five hundred more by then. *Original* words that will wow Mr. Mercer. My stomach knots at the possibility that he may very well read something *I've* written. How can I ever put words on paper that will impress a number-one *NYT* best seller—my fucking idol?

The first time I read one of his novels, I devoured it. Never had a story unfolded like that before. And his details—so graphic I had nightmares for *weeks*. His word choices, his characters, all perfect and fucked up. He possesses a gift that reveals the dark beauty, that carnal piece of humanity, that lives within all of us. Every single one of his works fills me with fascination, so how can I possibly write something up to that standard?

Stress mounts in my chest. Closing my eyes, I inhale. I massage my temples as I will my mind to come up with something. I would do just about anything for this position, and I swear to God, if Margaret Stanley's prissy little ass gets this collaboration...I'll kill her. My eyes pop wide, my lips twisting into a sly grin. If ever I had an idea that may get Mr. Mercer's attention, it's this.

An hour later, I have the perfect story of murder and mayhem, all centered around Mr. Mercer himself. The plot: a begrudged student who didn't win his contest kills the one who does. Simple. Genius. Compelling. Because maybe he'll worry I'll actually do it if he chooses someone other than me.

After I send the email to Ms. Barnes, I sigh. Right now, I have hope, and that's a feeling I rarely experience. Hope for a better life, for something that will set me apart from the rest of the monotonous, humdrum American society. This feeling, it's why people take risks. It's like that moment when you're holding fifty Megabucks tickets, waiting for them to announce the winning numbers. As long as you have those tickets, you can still daydream about all the ways you would squander your fortune.

———

It's late evening, and I'm alone at work. The best thing about this bookstore—the Little Novel Bookstore off Fifth and Main—is it's hidden away in a crappy part of town. Hardly anyone ever comes in here. There's only a single small window at the front, and once the sun goes down, the store becomes dim and gloomy, the perfect place for me to lose myself in my books. No people and a nice little reading retreat—well, it's the perfect place to work, isn't it?

The bell over the front door dings, prompting me to bookmark my spot in Mercer's *The Dark Deceit*. It's the fourth time I've read it, and it still makes my heart race as much as it did the first time. I peer over the cramped shelves. I see no one, but I hear the soles of their shoes padding over the tile floor.

I nervously clear my throat, pushing a bit higher on my tiptoes. My heart slams against my ribs as I frantically glance around to see who walked in and why they're hiding. I have a habit of letting my imagination get the better of me, as I'm told most writers do, and right now all I can think is that whoever just walked in is, at this very moment, pulling a wool ski mask over their nose as they slink around the self-help section. My pulse pounds harder with each beat because I'm now vividly imagining being tied up by this stranger and screaming for help just before he slits my throat open.

"Miranda?"

I spin around, trying to calm my ragged breathing.

Freckle-faced James stands in front of the counter, smiling. "Did my book come in yet?"

"Oh, um..." I shuffle through papers and invoices. "Um, no. Tomorrow maybe?"

STEVIE J. COLE & BT URRUELA

He nods. "You doing anything tonight?"

"Working."

"After you get off?"

I hate talking to people. I'm not good at it, and I try to avoid it at all costs. That's one reason I'm studying creative writing, one reason I choose to work at this run-down bookstore. I want as little interaction with the public as humanly possible because, in general, I don't trust people. Ninety-nine percent of them make me uncomfortable.

"After work I'm going home." I reopen my book to the marked page and begin reading, hoping he'll see I don't want to engage in conversation with him.

"Let me take you out or something."

"No." I don't look up from the page.

You see, this is what James does. He comes in once a week, orders some weird, retired title, then he tries to talk me into going out with him. He's quirky and ugly. His brown hair is always slicked back; his blue irises do nothing but accentuate how bloodshot his eyes are. And he always has this pungent odor. I think it's marijuana. At least that would explain the bloodshot eyes.

"Ah, come on, Miranda. I ask you out every week. Just go out with me once."

"Why, do you want to kill me or something?" I glare at him over the corner of page 172.

He rolls his beady little eyes. "No."

"You're strange, James."

"So are you." He runs his hand over his greasy hair. "Well, I'll come back tomorrow. For the book, you know?"

I nod, and a few seconds later, the bell over the front jingles as he leaves.

Some people give you that creepy Dahmer vibe, and James does that. Sometimes I think he's debating what herb best brings out the taste of human flesh: rosemary or sage. I'd go with rosemary.

An hour later, I'm halfway through chapter thirty when my cell phone rings. I glance at the screen but don't recognize the number. *Maybe it's Ms. Barnes calling to tell me I'm the student Mr. Mercer chose...*

"Hello?" I try to keep my voice from shaking.

"Baby," my mother slurs.

Closing my eyes, I exhale. "What do you need?"

"Some more money. I need some more money. The heater broke and..."

A man starts shouting in the background. Glass shatters.

"Can you help your momma out, baby?" She takes an audible drag of her cigarette. That noise alone makes the wretched smell of her Virginia Slims fill my nose. *How do smells do that?*

"I don't have any money. I sent you half of my last paycheck, and I told you I couldn't do that again."

"Hell, it was only fifty bucks." Another loud draw from her cigarette. "You got that fancy scholarship. You don't

STEVIE J. COLE & BT URRUELA

need no money."

"*Any* money. Basic grammar. It's *any* money." I groan, frustrated by the reminder of what shit I came from. "I can't help you. I'm sorry."

I hang up the phone and toss it into my backpack. Within a minute it's ringing again, so I turn it off.

Honestly, I don't know why I sent her the fifty dollars I did. She's a drunk. A drug addict. She was barely able to take care of me growing up. I've lived in cars, bathed in gas station sinks. When I was twelve, we moved into some run-down project housing on the outskirts of town, and I thought we were rich. The older I grew, the more I realized the only reason we lived the way we did was because my mother was a loser and couldn't hold down a job. But if you were to ask her, she'd blame me for her lot in life. She had me when she was fifteen, ran away from home. She "did the best she could." I roll my eyes as I hear her saying those exact words.

But the worst thing wasn't the fact that I lived off stale drive-thru food or went to ten different schools from first to fourth grade. No. The worst thing about growing up in poverty was the ridicule. I wore the same clothes damn near every day. I couldn't take regular showers or afford deodorant. And how do you think that worked out for an awkward, redheaded preteen? Well, how it worked out is one of the reasons I generally don't like people.

What people say to you, even if you hate them, it fucks

with your head. *Ugly. Smelly. Dumb.* So I didn't have friends. I didn't talk to anyone. I read, and eventually, I started writing. It was an escape. Fiction was the only way I stayed sane. But I didn't read romances or fairy tales. Nope. I looked for the gritty, the perverse. The dark. Because those kinds of stories gave me hope that there were far worse things in life than what I was dealing with. And that's why Mercer's writings are my favorites. Compared to the things his characters go through, my life resembles a Disney film, complete with singing, enchanted animals.

I always find hope. And as long as Mr. Mercer hasn't chosen a student yet, I still have hope.

CHAPTER TWO
Edwin

"Don't Fear the Reaper"—Denmark + Winter

Sifting through the thousands of emails and short stories my assistant "handpicked" for me out of the tens of thousands we received leads me to two conclusions. One, this new generation of writers is a fucking joke... and two, I need a new fucking assistant.

Janine, my aforementioned assistant, has been entrenched in her position for years now, so her being replaced is a pipe dream. I only meet with her a few times a month, and even that's too much for me. I'd rather keep people at a distance, and that includes those who work for me.

A Princeton grad, Janine's not all dumb. Perhaps she really did choose the best submissions this country's top writing programs have to offer and my plans of finding a co-writer are just futile. I can't imagine working with a single one of these so-called writers recycling other people's stories into their own ten-page drivel. I've read some version of *Psycho* at least a hundred times already. Stephen King clones? Don't even get me started.

I pull up a blank email and angrily jab at the keys.

Janine,

I find it incredibly hard to believe that this is the best of the best. Am I losing my fucking mind here, or are you losing your touch?

- Your Unhappy Boss

And sent.

I couldn't give two fucks about her feelings. I refuse to read another word of this shit.

Almost immediately, Janine responds. She knows well enough, from her years working for me, that I *do not* wait around for a response. Phone alerts will *always* remain on and loud enough to wake the dead.

EA,

So sorry for the last few batches. Unfortunately, this seems to be the best of what's come in. I do have some good news though. I just read a fantastic story. Edwin, just read the name…

-Janine

I open the document and scroll down the title page, stopping immediately. I let the cursor flash over the name. Are my eyes deceiving me? *Miranda Cross… Miranda, Miranda, Miranda.* Oh, how the name sends a surge of adrenaline throughout my body, like the electric tingling you get beneath the skin when the dealer hands you a full house, when life calls out loud and clear, *Today, is your day!*

Miranda, to most, means nothing. It means nothing to those who don't value the art of the written word. Who don't appreciate the classics. Who can't appreciate quiet legends operating right beneath their noses.

Miranda, to me, is a way of life.

I was fifteen years old and just entering the world of tainted fantasies and dreams of carnage when I randomly stumbled onto *The Collector* by John Fowles at the public library. Another moment when everything seemed to line up perfectly.

The Collector, for you uneducated fucks, is about a man, Frederick Clegg, who collects butterflies as a hobby. They are his life. But eventually, they just aren't enough to quell his need to collect, to contain, to control. That's when he decides to take a girl he's been obsessed with for some time. After careful preparation, he drugs and kidnaps her before keeping her locked in his cellar in an attempt to make her fall in love with him.

The name of that girl? *Miranda Grey.*

My obsession with the book led me to research everything about it. I found that many serial killers were equally obsessed with the book. Some even carried a copy with them on their murderous conquests. Eventually, my research led me to the Holy Grail, the inspiration for my kill shed, and the reason EA Mercer is splattered on best-seller lists across the world—Leonard Lake and Charles Ng.

Lake and Ng saw the beauty in *The Collector* just as I do. They respected and appreciated the need, the yearning, the ultimate desire to control other people. They understood that, as a stronger, smarter human being, it is our prerogative—no, our duty—to rid the world of lesser humans. To take what we wish and do what we want with it. We are the masters. They are the slaves.

Lake and Ng built their own kill shed in the wooded mountains of California, where they tortured, raped, and killed women, all while taping their endeavors. Sometimes they killed whole families to get rid of witnesses. The tapes, I sadly have never been able to get my hands on. However, Ng drew a few of the murders in almost childlike fashion, with crayons and jagged, uneven lines. One of them depicted him placing a baby over a burning charcoal grill. Not my style, per se, but inspiring nonetheless!

Yes, Miranda Cross will do just fine. Now it's time to see if her story carries any weight. But if I have to guess, I imagine it will knock me right on my ass. The universe lines itself up for me sometimes, and when it does, nothing can stop me.

CHAPTER THREE
Miranda

"Goner"—Twenty-One Pilots

Jesus Christ...

The pain radiates from my toe to my ankle, all the way to my shin.

"Fuck!" I hop on one foot, holding the other as I take several deep breaths in an attempt to make the pain subside. I glare at the corner of the dresser where I stubbed my toe. *Dumb piece of fucking furniture.*

I can't stop my body from shaking or myself from sweating. I've tried three times to put on eyeliner. But due to my unsteady hand, I've made a mess of it and had to wash off this ridiculous makeup twice. I've never been one to pile on cosmetics. I don't see the point. All of it is a lie. It's for vain girls with nothing inside their heads, for shallow people who only have their looks. Think about the damn word makeup. To *make up* for something you lack. Yet, here I sit in front of my mirror, attempting to draw a perfect thin black line around my round eyes.

And why?

Because in precisely two hours, twenty-seven minutes, and fifteen seconds—give or take a few—I'll be face-to-face with EA Mercer. Just the thought makes a large lump form in my throat. I swallow around it. *Around* it because it won't budge.

How many people get to have coffee with their idol, with the person who helped them ignore the shitty environment they grew up in? With the person who influenced their decision of what to do with their otherwise seemingly doomed existence?

Calm down, Miranda. Using my left hand, I steady my right and slowly, carefully—*successfully*—manage to line my eyes.

Once I finish applying my face, I step back and stare at my reflection. Pale skin. Hazel eyes framed in thick made-up lashes. As I stare at myself, I can't help but think that with all this shit on my face, I actually look like a 1940s pinup. Nice dress. New shoes I bought on credit. Full face of flawless makeup. I look completely put together, girly, and possibly sociable. Oh, how fake first impressions can be. But if there's one thing I've learned in life, it's that impressions determine everything.

Really, *looks* determine everything. No one cares if you're smart or nice or caring. No. People care, first and foremost, about your appearance. And for the first time in my life, as I take in the stunning redhead in the mirror with polished nails and a trim waist, I believe that my looks might possibly *help* me.

Just before I turn to leave, I coat my full lips with a bright red lipstick that reminds me of Marilyn Monroe. After all, the one thing I've learned from reading each of Mr. Mercer's books a minimum of four times is that he has a penchant for an hourglass figure and a redhead with slut-red lips.

———

"Would you like more water?" the gangly waiter asks for the second time in five minutes.

I force a smile and shake my head. "No, thank you though."

I glance at the dainty antique watch on my wrist. Five minutes overdue. I tap my foot on the floor of the empty coffee shop. Clasping the glass with both hands, I go over the possible questions he may ask me. *What are your goals as a writer?* To be you. *What made you decide to write?* You. *Who is your favorite author?* You. You. You!

I clear my throat and remind myself to not answer "you" to everything or else I may scare him. After all, I can't have him thinking I'm some crazy, obsessed fan. I'm not. I'm a reader—no, I'm a writer. A writer, not a stalker.

I swallow around that lump once more, and as I do, a shadow falls over the table—a shadow that sends chill bumps scattering over my skin. Slowly, I glance up, my pulse steadily picking up as my gaze scans up a pair of jeans to a freshly pressed dark gray shirt, to the face of the man who changed my whole world. This man's mind is beautifully mad, and the worst part about this meeting is that I now realize he may be just as beautiful physically as he is mentally. Tanned skin. Dark, impossibly bottomless eyes. Thick, messy brown hair. It's enough to make even me—a girl who cares nothing at all for men—swoon.

And swoon I fucking do. My mouth is suddenly dry, my mind a jumbled mess. Sweat slicks my skin, and my head spins. For a brief moment, I fear the sheer delight from being so damn close to him may make me faint. I manage a polite smile, fighting to keep it from spreading all the way across my face.

"Mr. Mercer," I say, holding out my hand.

Everything seems to move in slow motion, and my pulse goes crazy at the thought that I am actually about to touch him.

He stops several feet in front of the table, glaring at me, but he doesn't take my outstretched hand. His eyes narrow slightly, and I break out into a sweat. The smile quickly fades from my face. Without a word, he pulls out the chair across from me. The second he sits, he snaps his fingers at the barista then redirects his attention to me. He's not actually looking at me—no, he's *studying* me like an opponent sizing up the rival they know they'll too easily knock to the ground. I anxiously drum my fingers over the table and clear my throat as I wonder what the hell I've gotten myself into.

"Ms. Cross, I must say I appreciate your timeliness. There's nothing that pisses me off more than someone who's late for a meeting. So for that, I thank you." His eyes never leave mine, and it's both intimidating and unnervingly sexy.

Never in my life did I think I'd be sitting across from EA Mercer. I try my best to stifle the sweat beginning to creep down my forehead.

"Thank *you*, Mr. Mercer. I..." I take a breath. I remind myself to remain collected even though every muscle in my body is ready to give out. "It's such an honor to even be considered for this opportunity. I—"

The barista stops at the end of the table and stares at us.

Edwin looks at me, annoyance etched on his face. "Coffee. Black. Ms. Cross, have you ordered already?"

"Miranda, please." I shoot a smile at Edwin before I glance at the barista. "I'll just stick with my water."

A nervous smile forms on the barista's face as he nods and scurries off. I don't blame him. Mr. Mercer is intimidating.

"So how much do you know about what I'm looking for here? I realize I didn't give much guidance, but you do understand whomever I choose will be co-writing my next novel—potentially ghostwriting," he says with a sliver of arrogance to his tone.

"Uh, yes." My heart rate accelerates. "I knew about the co-writing bit, of course, the contest and all. I think that was clear in the email, but I, uh, I wasn't aware it may be ghostwriting..." I ramble, telling myself to shut the hell up.

Edwin straightens, narrowing his eyes on me. "And is that a problem? You do understand the opportunity I'm presenting, correct?"

My mouth has suddenly gone dry. "Yes, I absolutely do, and I didn't mean for that to sound, um, I didn't mean for it to sound..." *Shit. Get it together, Miranda.* "I didn't mean for it to sound unappreciative. I'd love *any* opportunity to write with you, Mr. Mercer."

"Good." His dark eyes lock with mine in the most intense stare I've possibly ever witnessed. "Very good... because I liked your story, Miranda. I don't like many other people's work, and after the thousands of shit stories from your peers my assistant sent over the past month, yours certainly stood out."

Edwin's stare remains glued to mine.

A smile tears at my lips. "Thank you very much for—"

"Don't thank me. I'm not one for doling out compliments. I find them pointless. I am only stating a fact. You still need a lot of work, but I think the potential is there. I'm not set on who I will choose just yet—or whether or not I'll choose anyone at all. This is not something I wanted to do. Not by a long shot," he scoffs.

And what do you say to that? What kind of response

could I possibly give to that? While I assumed he'd be arrogant, I didn't think he'd be rude. He almost seems disgusted by the idea of co-writing with someone, which does take away from the appeal, but no amount of arrogance in the world could make me step away from this opportunity.

"The fact that you see any potential with my work at all, honestly, is enough. I've read every single one of your books—several times—and you're a genius with words. So whether you decide to go any further than this right here, well..." I nervously drum my fingers over the tabletop, and he smirks. Something in that smirk makes me uneasy.

"That's what I like to hear. My publisher wants this book by December. That means we have a little over two months. While I don't often meet anyone's deadline but my own, I would like to get started on this book right away. If you are chosen, I would ask that you come out to my cabin to work. Whether you have school or not, this *is* the timeline. Would that be an issue?"

"Not at all." I shake my head. "I can take the fall semester off."

He stands. "Well, Miranda, my assistant will be in touch *if* I decide to work with you. Have a good day."

He turns on his heel, slipping his jacket on, and walks briskly for the door. My mouth gapes. I know I should say something, but his sudden departure has me at a loss for words. *Did I really just come all the way out here for this?*

I stand abruptly, the legs of my chair scraping over the floor. "Thanks, Mr. Mercer. It was nice to meet you," I call feebly, shaking my head at how stupid I sound.

Of course he doesn't respond or even turn. He simply continues toward the door, leaving me standing in an uncomfortable silence.

CHAPTER FOUR
Edwin

"Closer"—Nine Inch Nails

A gust of wind blows, leaves swirling in its wake. Another angry puff from the storm brewing, and the cold autumn rain slaps against my window. I stare mindlessly at the blinking cursor and blank page, my fingers tapping my antique mahogany desk. I write prologues that stick with you. They pull you in, beat the ever-loving shit out of you, and leave you begging for more. That's not an easy feat— even for someone with my skill.

I just can't seem to get the words out. They're right on the tip of my tongue, but just as all my other novels have started, so does this one—the words coming out in a big pile of steaming shit. Writer's block is not new to me, but the first page... the first page is a real bitch.

And Miranda. *Fucking* Miranda Cross. The woman hasn't left my mind since I left her at the coffee shop two days ago. Her talent is undeniable, though she'll never hear me say it, but I don't know if that's why she's taken up residence in my brain or if it's because fate seems to be wrapping its hands tightly around my neck.

She's beautiful, no doubt about that. I'd be lying if I said that hadn't taken me by complete surprise. Her story was good. *Really* good. And from the ruthlessness of it, I would've never expected someone so timid and beautiful. Beautiful women don't struggle. Beauty is like a free pass through life.

I pull her manuscript from my desk drawer. I turn to the climax and pour over her words once more:

I grip the handle of the hunting knife in my right hand. That woman is to blame for the way my life unraveled like loose thread. She's selfish. She took what should have been mine. She drove me to this. Really, she did, so it's fine that I don't feel guilty as I step to the edge of her bed and envision plunging this blade so deeply into her chest that it pins her to the fucking mattress. My pulse skips a few beats. My skin buzzes with excitement.

Without a flicker of hesitation, I quickly jab the knife into her side then pull it out. It feels just like stabbing a ripe pumpkin. And oh, does she fucking wail. Wakes up with a jolt and a high-pitched scream. She's balled up, clutching her side, not even paying attention to me standing at the side of her bed.

I laugh deep in my throat and lean over the mattress. Fisting her blond ponytail, I yank her face toward mine. "Shhh, Marian. Shhh."

She fights me, scratching and shouting, punching, but she's weak. She's losing a lot of blood. I know because I can hear it drip—drip—drip *from the bed to the floor. Not to mention my jeans are soaked with it.*

I climb onto the bed and straddle her as I grab her right arm. "Now, I do believe I remember..." I say as I rotate her arm clockwise then snap her shoulder out of socket with a more-than-pleasing pop.

And fuck me if she doesn't scream even louder. I slam my free hand—the one with the blood-stained knife—over her mouth to quiet her pathetic cries for help.

"Remember how you said that little move was ridiculous in my essay, hmmm, do you?" I smirk because this serves her smart ass right. She was wrong. I was right. "I am going to show you just how authentic that little story was."

Her eyes go wide with fear, tears spilling down her cheeks as she shakes her head. I move my hand away from her mouth then press the blade beneath her chin, slowly dragging it down to the center of her windpipe. She thrashes about, crying again, which does nothing but annoy me. She's going to die, and the sooner she makes peace with that, the easier this will be for us both. It's not like I like her screaming; I just want her to shut up. That's all I've ever wanted was for her to just shut the fuck up.

Having had enough, I watch with curiosity as I press the knife ever so slowly over her porcelain skin. A little more force and the skin breaks—almost pops. A thin line of blood seeps around the blade, and I can't help it—I want to see more.

I press the blade against her neck a little harder, and I'm rewarded with more blood and, of course, more of Marian's pleas to a God who will never hear her. I drag the knife across her throat, and a beautifully perfect, pulsing crimson line appears. Her cries grow softer. Gurgling. She's choking. After a few seconds, she falls silent.

Inhaling, I relish the silence as I stare at her lifeless figure, but there's something inside me—some bloodlust— that says it's not quite done yet. I just want to know what it would feel like to take her head off, that's all. Curiosity. I just wonder what it feels like.

I cut through her flesh over and over. Almost in a frenzy, I slice through the muscles and tendons. Funny the different levels of force one must use to tear through cartilage. And the amount of blood is unimaginable. The white sheets are drenched with it. My hands are slick with the sticky fluid.

For some unknown reason, I want her head. It has to be off. It's an impulse, so I keep hacking away until the blade hits her vertebrae. Narrowing my eyes, I focus on the task at hand and use short, quick strokes to sever the tiny bones. It's almost loose. I can see it. I grab onto her hair and pull, then I give one final slash, and her head is freed with a delightfully wet pop.

Smiling, I hold it up as I glare into her glassy eyes that will never again close.

"My story was better. My words were better, Marian," I whisper before climbing off the bed. I tuck her head beneath my arm as I make my way toward the door.

A smile works over my lips as I stash the story safely away in my top desk drawer. This girl must have demons in her past. I like that. I like that very much.

I'm still not sure about her, but with every new craptastic story that comes in, I'm leaning more and more toward bringing her on. It's like I don't have any real option. This was meant to be. It must be.

Out of nowhere, the words start to come. They pour from my mind and through my fingers so fast I can hardly keep up. My male lead has a woman chained to a dingy bed. Her mouth is duct-taped. Her eyes billow with tears as they beg my lead for mercy—*Miranda* begs for mercy. I have my muse.

As I write with the purpose of drawing my readers into my fucked up world, I think about what it will be like to actually kill Miranda when this is all said and done. How delightful it will be to see those beautiful hazel eyes come to full realization as I unleash my hell on her. I may even keep her for longer than a week after the writing's all finished. Perhaps, like my hero Mr. Clegg, I'll keep this specimen a long while. Maybe I'll keep her forever.

It isn't long, maybe four or five pages, before the block comes again; the words jumble in my head, losing all meaning by the time they hit the screen. My stomach tightens, churning in disgust and oncoming rage, but I fight it back. I've been right here far too many times before to let it control me anymore.

I got four decent pages at least. Shit, some of it may even be spared the delete key. That's enough for me to let the desire win. I'm overwhelmed by it. I yearn to fuck... and to kill.

But I never kill what I fuck.

Call it not shitting where I eat, I guess, but I have a prostitute out of Asheville I always use. Chastity likes to get fucked... and she likes to get fucked hard. Her tears are very real as I choke her half to death, simultaneously slamming my cock into her, but she gets off on it every single time. She begs me for it. Half the time she doesn't even charge me. And then, after her, I find my prey.

I grab my leather coat from the chair back and my beanie from the bookcase, pulling the hat on as I head for my office closet. I open the closet door, exposing my gun safe. With a quick spin of the combination lock—0-4-2-0-1-1, the date of my first murder—the solid steel door creaks open. Inside are my guns, twenty of them and of all varieties, along with three identical briefcases tucked neatly at the bottom of the safe. I crouch and grab the first one, which contains my bind-fuck-kill kit. I don't even need to check if it's the right one. I've been doing this a while.

Closing the safe and closet doors, I make my way through the cabin hallway to my front door. My body is buzzing. The adrenaline has kicked in, sending a charge up and down my arms and legs. I'm ready for this. And even though I have an hour's drive ahead of me, this feeling won't change. When I'm on the prowl, I'm at my best. I conquer the world one miserable soul at a time.

My first stop is Taylor, NC, about thirty minutes from my cabin. It's a quiet, dreadful little town full of redneck fucks I'd rather not mingle with, but one of those fucks is an old high school friend—if I've ever had such a thing as friends. He runs a Ride Spot Rent-A-Car out of Taylor. He gives me good deals, doesn't ask questions, and rents to me whenever I damn well please. Being a well-known author, my name carries weight around this entire fucking world. Now imagine how it is with those I grew up with. It's not hard for me to make shit happen.

He rents me a little Chevy Sonic.

"Business in Myrtle Beach," I tell him.

"Been there once. Fucked three strippers," he responds.

After a quick cash transaction, I'm on the road again and ready. Ready to take on the night. Ready to unleash some carnage. Ready to fuck some shit up.

Asheville isn't the quaint little Southern city it once was. Many of these desperate city streets, ones I've become quite familiar with, are now places normal people like to ignore. They're the gum on the bottom of your shoe. They're straight out of fucking Hollywood. For me, they're like a drug. I feel comfort in the darkness... in the silence.

I park next to a curb, drawing the attention of a few bums huddled along some buildings, but most stay bundled tightly in moving blankets and newspaper. I shoot off a quick page to Chastity, my only method of communication with her—the only one I want to use, that is—and after a few moments, she comes slinking from the alleyway in her usual yoga pants, Nike running shoes, and black pullover, her arms folded tightly against her petite body. She pulls the handle and jumps quickly into the passenger seat, putting both hands to the vents.

"Don't you own a jacket, woman?" I ask as she looks at me, her nose and ears bright red, skin flushed, and bottom lip clenched between chattering teeth. I pull away as she finally begins to warm up.

Her shivering calms. "I didn't think it would be this cold. It's only a few flights of stairs and a ten-foot walk, but damn, I think my pussy froze off." She laughs.

"I guess I'm destroying your asshole then?" I shoot her a smirk, and her eyes instantly widen.

She shakes her head slowly, her long blond hair swinging from side to side, her arms still mummy-like against the vents. "Please, no, I think she's gonna be just fine." She laughs again, patting her groin and sliding her other hand against my leg. She gives my thigh two good squeezes. "I've missed you."

"Honey," I say as I pull into our usual motel, "Well, I can't say the same, but I can say I've missed *fucking* you." My dick twitches at the thought of cuffing her hands and feet to the bed frame and taking her for everything she's worth.

"You have no idea. I've had so many fucking old rich fucks lately who want me to peg their assholes. I just don't get it," she says.

My nose scrunches in disgust as I put the car in park. "Well, my beautiful little slut"—I grab her hair and pull her face closer to mine—"I hope you didn't bring your strap-on tonight because you certainly won't be needing it."

I kiss her hard, taking her bottom lip between my teeth and pulling back almost enough to break skin. She whimpers before our lips connect again. I tear away, letting go of her hair. Her eyes remain closed, her head drifting slightly from side to side.

"I can promise you that." I smile and pop the door open.

"Now *that* I've missed," she says, opening her eyes, a broad smile taking up her face.

I lean toward the backseat, grab my briefcase, and step out of the car before looking back in at her. "Don't go expecting much of that. Don't you even think about it." I pass her an evil smirk and close the door just as she attempts to respond.

Have you ever had a moment when you were in complete control? When the world felt as if it were just a marble in your balled up fist? That's how I feel when I fuck and when I kill. This is my hour. This is my calling. I am the god of fuck, and I do the Devil's dirty work, and tonight, my wrath will be felt.

———

Each of Chastity's slender limbs are cuffed to the bed frame. She looks beautiful spread out in an X, blindfolded, gagged, and facedown on a mattress yellowed with age. A dim glow is cast around the room by the few large candles on the cheap desk. I take one in my hand. I can hear her force thick, wet breaths around the ball gag as I inch closer to her, steadying the burning candle. She knows nothing about what's to come. She never does.

With a quick flick of my wrist, a smattering of melted wax plops against her back and ass. She gasps, her hands gripping the cuffs so tight it looks as though her ligaments may rupture her skin at any moment. Another flick of the wrist and she lets out a muffled scream. Her body curls in pain.

"Shut up, Chastity!" I say with a growl, placing the candle back on the desk.

I rub my palm over the curve of her ass before smacking it hard. A red handprint slowly rises to the surface of her pale skin, and I smile. I want to hurt her. I want her to scream until those worthless fucking tears of hers spill down her cheeks.

The thought of those tears nearly drives me to the brink of madness, and I quickly pull down my jeans, grabbing my cock and fisting it as I loosen the restraints around her legs. Stepping behind her, I grab her hips, my fingers digging into her flesh as I yank her ass into the air. Sometimes I wonder if I could grip her hard enough to tear her flesh open, but I won't do that tonight. I'll save that for next time—maybe.

I press my left hand over the small of her back, forcing it down into the mattress as I rub a single finger over her pussy, exposed and waiting for me to do with it as I fucking please.

"Remember. Don't fucking move." I place my cock against her then grab her hair and yank her head as I lay over her, placing my lips by her ear. "And don't make a goddamn sound. Play dead, my little slut."

I slam into her, burying myself to the hilt. She is completely under my control, and though her cries sound as though she's in agony, she's loving every fucking minute of this. She craves receiving pain just as I crave giving it to her. Right now, I own her, bought and paid for. I am reinventing her, using her, and the thought that, if I wanted to, I could kill her with my bare hands... well, that makes me fuck her even harder.

I wrap my hand around her neck, and with each

powerful thrust of my cock, I squeeze just a little tighter. She gags and chokes, and I let up, wanting to crush her throat but knowing now is not the time. The temptation is there though—but then again, when isn't it? I fight the urge to end her because I like making her come, making her moan, and all at the touch of a murderer.

It's my dirty little secret, my wicked little lie.

An hour later, I drop Chastity off in front of a 7-Eleven, and with a screech of tires against the pavement, my night truly begins. If it goes according to plan, this evening will come to a close on Tenth Street.

CHAPTER FIVE

Jackson

"Creep"—Radiohead

I'm a sad, pathetic little fuck—it's all I can think as I stare at my reflection in the mirror.

Now, I know that's probably not something you're likely to hear from most thirty-somethings who are fit and possess a legitimate career. Something more than "entrepreneur," that is. But for me, it's an intrusive thought that takes over from the moment I wake. Blame me if you want, but I was programmed this way.

The morning news spouts the usual depressing bullshit in the background as I sip my coffee and Jameson, half ignoring what I'll get to experience firsthand shortly. I've been a homicide detective with Asheville's police department for four years now. I served three tough years in the army before that. I've seen the worst this world has to offer, and I live it every single day through victims and heartbroken family members, through the carnage and bloodshed.

I rub a hand through my uncombed hair. The ever-present tired look in my eye staring back at me from the mirror is a nice reminder that being a detective takes the life right out of you. That's not the only thing sucking the life out of me, of course. My childhood comes into play quite often. My time in the army also consumes my thoughts, playing out like fucked up home movies in my dreams.

Sometimes I look back and wish I could change things. I wish I could erase the war, erase the pain of growing up broken. But more often than not, I'm resigned to a sense of understanding. I've made my peace with the Lord, however broken that peace may be. I'm his factory defect. I try my best to fight the absurd carnival of torment inside my mind, but alas, it's a twenty-four-seven party.

———

The unusual bustle of the department at seven in the morning lets me know I'm in for a treat today. I'm one of only a handful of detectives around when I arrive most mornings, and I'm always the first one in from the day shift. As I reach my office and toss my briefcase onto the desk, my partner, Detective Tommy Matthews, appears in the doorway. He raps two knuckles against the doorframe and lifts a manila folder, shaking his head.

"Let me fuckin' guess," I huff as I sit in the stiff leather chair. "Another cold one?"

"You got it. Two units found her around 3 a.m., dumped in an abandoned house down on Tenth Street." Tommy tosses the folder on the desk in front of me and takes a seat himself. "It was a fresh one. Cold maybe three hours."

"Tenth Street? Go figure. Is it our guy?" I flip the folder open, grab a pair of reading glasses from the desk, and slide them onto the bridge of my nose. I only hold the folder for now, peering over the top of my glasses at my partner and waiting for a response.

"Sure looks like it. Tortured and his signature Xs. When Joe called me this morning asking if I could come in early, he said he could tell right away this was our guy. Either that or a real good copycat." He motions to the folder, drawing my eyes to it. "If you'll look at the pics he took and the report, you'll see what I mean."

I scan the information and see a picture of a woman, shirtless with jean shorts hiked down to her ankles. Her hands are bound with her own bra. A mess of duct tape is wrapped around her eyes and nose.

"She was bound the same way," he says. "No rape, but looks like some real fucked up shit was done to her before she died. And like I said, she was marked like the others. We got the examiner looking at her now."

Her face is beaten beyond recognition. Each breast is engraved with a deep, bloody X, the nipples removed. I flip the picture and review Joe's report.

47

Tommy continues as I read. "Twenty-seven, no immediate family, a dozen or so prostitution arrests. The last one was just two months ago. This is our fucking guy, Jax. Or a real good fucking imitator."

"Is Joe going to let us in on this one or be a prick as usual?" I ask, knowing full well our dear Detective Sanders is a bit of a hoarder when it comes to big cases. He detests sharing credit.

"You know with any other case he would've bitched up a storm and probably kept us as far away as possible, but he knows this guy's yours. He knows what the case means to you. Besides that, Chief Wentz knows what the case means to you. I don't think Joe's going to fuck with that," Tommy says, much to my relief. He motions to the book on my desk, the latest best seller from my all-time favorite author, EA Mercer. "How do you even read that shit? Considering what we do for a living, you don't get enough murder and mayhem on the job?"

"What can I say, man? The guy changed my life. He's the reason I became a cop. Besides, he's a North Carolina treasure," I say as my mind drifts to my college days, which seem so long ago.

I got out of the army without a clue of what I wanted to do. I went to some shit college to be a financial planner or some nine-to-five bullshit like that. Picked up one of his books one day, and I fell in love. I wanted to be one of the detectives from his novels, catching the cocksuckers that now take up my every thought. Their crimes are a morbid tapestry in my brain.

I smile, raising my palms to show off my pint-size office. "And the rest is history. Now I'm the made man you see before you."

Tommy grins and shakes his head. "You sure you ain't regretting changing your degree? A recent college grad on the arm and a Benz in the drive don't sound half bad." He scans the tiled ceiling and blinding fluorescent lights as if in thought. He shakes his head again. "Yeah, real fuckin' good."

"Shit, at least you got a wife and kid. You're smart— you got married in college. Trying to find a wife after getting in this field? Not fuckin' happening."

"Riiiight, like you even try, Peralta. When's the last time you had a damn girlfriend?" he asks, his face scrunched in wonder. "Last time you went on a date even?"

"Longer than I can remember, my friend. Now, don't we have more important shit to do than talk about my love life?" I say, waving the folder at him.

"I suppose so, but let me know any time you wanna take the wife and kid for a weekend or year or whatever!" He flashes a cheesy grin below his Tom Selleck mustache.

"I'm gonna have to pass."

"Well, it's a standing offer, partner." He laughs, putting his hands on his impressive beginner's beer gut.

Ten years my senior, the donuts and therapy beer

have caught up to him. Then again, he probably hasn't seen a gym in a few years. He always says it's elbow tendonitis acting up. Mr. Excuse is what I call him. Like me, he joined the department at an older age than most. I thought getting into this gig at twenty-six was tough; I can't imagine doing it at thirty-two. But he's a funny, hard-working old bastard and a damn good partner.

"I'm gonna go ahead and give you a forever hard pass then." I laugh, running my fingers through my damp hair. My office runs furnace-hot, so I'm in a constant state of sweat. "So we have eight identical murders now with this guy and another three that look awfully similar." I open the file again, jostling through the top few pages. "All arrested for prostitution—"

"And about one or two more disappearing every few months... and that's just in Asheville," Tommy interjects. "We know he's operated elsewhere."

"Exactly. He's precise. He's smart. Leaves no evidence. Some found dead for mere hours, others for weeks, but no sexual assault with any of the victims. So why keep them?"

"They're his trophies. Maybe he gets off on the power. Who knows, man? You know how these motherfuckers are. There's no rhyme or reason to it."

"But that's where I think you're wrong, my friend," I say, closing the file and stuffing it into my briefcase. "I think there is a pattern to it. It's a game he's playing. And I get the feeling he knows exactly what he's doing." I stand, remove my coat from the rack, and slip it on. "Let's go down to Tenth Street and talk to some of the regulars. See if they've seen anything strange with any of their Johns. We can swing by the crime scene too."

Tommy stands too, rubbing his hands together. "Hooker patrol, let's do it! I'll get the car warmed up."

He turns and heads out the door. I don't move right away. Instead I let the four years I've spent chasing this killer wash over me in a flood of fucked up reminiscence. Four years of torture, mutilation, and death. Four years of missed chances and blown opportunities. I'm still no closer to catching him than the day I started, but it's what drives me.

That—and this motherfucker killed my baby sister. For that, he will be caught. It's just a matter of when.

CHAPTER SIX
Miranda

"Pretty Monster"—Reckless Serenade

Thirty minutes ago, the taxi pulled off the main highway onto this narrow side road. I always feel so awkward in the back of a cab. Do you attempt to strike up a conversation with the driver or not? It feels rude not to but overly friendly if you do. I decide to keep quiet, resting my forehead against the window as I watch the turning autumn trees whizz past.

Am I excited? Of course. Excited. Nervous—no, I'm terrified. Mr. Mercer chose *me* out of all the applicants—not fucking Margaret Stanley. But what does that mean anyway?

To say he left me unnerved at the coffee shop is an understatement. There is something about him, something deep-seated within him—in his eyes—that scares me a little. Maybe it's arrogance or intelligence or my own obsession with him, but something about him leaves me utterly mortified to be in his presence, yet here I am on my way to his cabin to write an entire novel *alongside* him. It makes my stomach kink. I'm worried he'll realize on day one what a shitty writer I am and send me packing. I debated asking if we could do this co-author deal via email or fucking Google docs, but after thinking that over, I figured it would only aggravate him if I asked. For some reason, I think he may have *very* little patience.

The cab takes a sharp right turn, and begins weaving up a twisting mountain ridge. The farther up we go, the thicker the trees grow, and a slight drizzle begins to fall. The driver flicks a knob on the steering wheel, and the windshield wipers screech over the glass. The noise makes my skin prickle. My phone buzzes, and when I see it's my mother, I press Ignore. The last thing I want her to know is that I'm here. She'll see it as her jackpot.

"Hell, this is out in the middle of nowhere, huh?" the pudgy man crammed into the driver's seat mumbles.

"Yeah..."

He chuckles. "Why'd the hell would somebody want to live this far from town? They killing people or somethin'?"

Chill bumps sweep over my skin, and I laugh to ease the tension. "Maybe." *Maybe...*

After driving several miles up the mountain in silence, we turn onto a one-lane road. I can barely see the outline of the road from the pile of leaves covering it. Woods. Thick woods surround us for a good five minutes before the taxi rolls to a stop, brakes squeaking. I glance out of the window at a small cabin, my breath fogging over the glass. My brow wrinkles. I'd expected something more... extravagant. Edwin Mercer is a eight-time number-one *NYT* best-selling author. He's made millions of dollars, and this—I narrow my gaze at the log cabin with smoke billowing from the stone chimney—*this* is what he lives in? Almost immediately, I chastise myself. *Simplicity.* That's respectable.

I pay the driver, grab my luggage from the back, and slam the trunk. The tires crunch over gravel as he pulls away, and once the hum of the engine disappears down the road, I realize how silent it is out here.

I glance at the thick woods lining his property. I can just make out a tiny shed nestled by the tree line. My heart rate kicks up a notch, and I'm not even sure why I have this apprehension—it's only my entire future that hinges upon this project.

The wind picks up, shaking a few leaves from the tree limbs, and I shiver. The late-autumn air has a nasty chill to it. I hate cold like this. It reminds me of being a kid in that scummy apartment without any heat, unable to sleep because I couldn't stop shaking. It reminds me of how much I hate my mother... just thinking about her sends my pulse into overdrive. Closing my eyes, I take a deep breath and push my shoulders back. A moment later, I slowly walk toward the cabin, struggling to drag my luggage over the uneven ground.

The porch creaks when I step onto it. Even though it's rather cold outside, sweat builds under my hair and slicks my palms as I stare at the worn door, reciting what I'll say to him. I manage to calm myself and timidly knock.

The doorknob turns, the hinges to the door groaning when Mr. Mercer yanks it open. "Welcome, Ms. Cross. Did the driver have any trouble finding the place?"

"No," I say, stepping into the massive living room. It's much more spacious than the outside makes it appear.

"Well, that's a first. Those fucks can never get it right." He takes the luggage from my hand and sets it to the side, putting a hand up to welcome me in.

This—*this* is not simplicity. Everything is immaculate and orderly. The tongue-and-groove ceiling meets in a peak. The room is completely open. All of the leather furniture looks unused. The hardwood floors gleam under the midafternoon sun pouring in from the large bay window at the back of the room. Expensive-looking art hangs neatly on the walls. Above the large stone fireplace, with its roaring fire, are several proudly mounted animal heads, their lifeless eyes glaring at me. My gaze drifts around the room again, stopping on that huge window.

Edwin cocks his head, a slight smile tugging at the corner of his lips. "I see you've spotted the impeccable view. That view is the *exact* reason I bought the place."

I nod because I don't know what else to do. He makes me nervous. I'm afraid no matter what I say, I'll sound like a bumbling idiot.

"Let's check it out first then. It's where we'll be spending the majority of our time anyway." He nods toward the opposite side of the room. "After you."

I hesitate before starting toward the large desk positioned in front of the window, Edwin close behind me. Nearly to the desk, my foot catches on the large area rug, and I stumble, my arms flailing gracelessly as I attempt to stop myself. But I don't need to stop myself, because Edwin catches me just before I fall into the desk, his strong hands tightly gripping my hips to steady me.

The heat of embarrassment washes over me as my eyes rise to meet his. "Thank you," I whisper.

His gaze strays to my lips for the briefest moment, then he releases me. He walks to the desk, stopping in front of it, and peers out of the window.

He looks flustered. "So..." He clears his throat. "This is my pride and joy. Every best seller I've ever written has been done right here." He motions toward the window. "Looking out at *that*."

The view *is* breathtaking. There's a large lot of flat land, but just beyond that lie miles and miles of thick woods. In the distance, mountains rise against the horizon. The autumn woods are a sea of burnt oranges and deep reds against a bright blue sky. Nothing but nature as far as I can see. No distractions, just natural beauty. I can see why this inspires him.

STEVIE J. COLE & BT URRUELA

I glance at Edwin to compliment the view, but he's still staring out of the window, almost in a daze. Following his gaze, I find it aimed at the shed at the edge of the property, just before the thick tree line begins. The construction looks fairly new. Most of it is built from wood. The roof is tin, and the metal door has a visibly large latch on the outside. It reminds me of those bomb shelters paranoid people built in the '50s, and I wouldn't doubt that a man like him built it for such an occasion. Writers are a strange breed. After all, we hear voices in our heads all the time, and sometimes, we even talk to them as though they're real...

Edwin's gaze moves from the window to me, his eyes locking on mine as he runs a thick finger against the mahogany desk. "I had my assistant, Janine, set up your workstation for you. I'm sure you'll find it more than adequate."

On the desk are two computers. Side by side. This man—this *New York Times* best-selling author—wants me to sit elbow to elbow with him while I write? My stomach knots, and sweat pricks over my forehead. How in the hell am I supposed to write with him glaring over my shoulder?

"Thanks," I say with a fake smile to hide my apprehension. "It looks perfect."

"Good. Speaking of Janine," he says, walking out of the office and back through the living room. He looks over his shoulder. "She stays in the city. If you need anything, I left her number on your pillow. Dietary restrictions, rides to the city, what have you... that's the kind of shit she can take care of."

For some reason, when he swears like that, I find it abrasive. Maybe it's because he's rather eloquent, or maybe it's my preconceived notion of him—the one where he was without flaw, almost godlike, because idols are rarely human. He's not at all like I imagined, and if I'm honest, I rather like that.

He continues to a hallway to the left of the front door and turns to me. "I write impulsively and at very random times. That's why it's best that you stay here." He motions down the hall. "Yours will be the room on the left."

I follow him down the narrow corridor, curiously looking into each open doorway. Just across from my room is what I assume is his. The four-poster king-size bed is neatly made. The curtains over the windows on either side of the bed are drawn, leaving the room in a sullen darkness. That's where he sleeps... and fucks.

I take a quick look at him, my eyes drifting down his body. He writes some messed up shit. The sex is always degrading and rough. Animalistic and raw. I can't help but imagine he must be filthy. He probably ties women up to that bed—why else would you have a bed like that? I bet he binds them, spanks them, calls them all kinds of filthy names before he finally fucks them. I shouldn't wonder it, but I can't help myself—what would it be like to have EA Mercer inside you?

Clearing his throat, he stops in front of his bedroom door. I realize I've just been standing there, peering into his room. I feel like such a whore for having imagined him in such a way. I'm not a pervert. I'm not...

He narrows his eyes at me. I can see him studying me, possibly dissecting me bit by bit. It makes me uncomfortable because I want him to see me as a strong, intelligent woman, and I fear if he looks too hard, he'll see that I'm not.

Without a word, he starts inside his room but stops abruptly. Looking back, he holds up a finger. "Oh, and I'm not sure if you've checked yet, but don't even concern yourself with getting cell service out here. There is none." He points the same finger down the hall where we came from. "The house phone is in the kitchen."

"Oh, sure. Okay," I say.

A short-lived smile flinches over his lips before he turns, walks into his room, and shuts the door. Something in that grin leaves me unsettled. So much so that my hands are shaking when I open the door to my room. I'm miles away from the nearest city, in the middle of fucking nowhere, with a man I feel like I know. I *feel* like I know him because he's EA Mercer. He's famous. I've read his words—read article after article about him—but the thing is, I know absolutely *nothing* about him.

And I am staying in his cabin.

In the woods.

All alone.

I anxiously peer into the hallway as I slowly close my door, the unoiled hinges creaking. I stare at the handle, fighting with myself. Telling myself to stop being such a paranoid freak. To stop buying into all of the shit I read so much—convincing myself everything is fine. As soon as I turn from the door, my gaze strays out of the large window on the back wall, and all I can see is that shed. My heart rate kicks up as I spin back around, palms flat against the bedroom door.

I take a deep breath as I stare at the handle. I can't help it—I impulsively twist the lock and pull back on the door to check that it's secure before I turn toward the bed.

After all, someone who can conjure up the twisted shit he writes... how much can you really trust someone with an imagination like that?

———

I've been here three days, and we have a total of five thousand words. That's it. It's not easy to write with him next to me. Everything I write is wrong. He huffs and puffs over my "amateur" word choices, and to be honest, I've never met anyone quite so rude. He reminds me every chance he gets that I'm still in grad school and without a published book under my belt. Not to mention he likes to throw things when he gets really annoyed. The lamp. The keyboard. Coffee mugs. There's a nice stain on the wall beside me where he hurled his cup yesterday morning.

My fingers shake as I type out my sentence.

My heart races in my chest as I press my back against the cold, wooden door...

Edwin groans, tossing his head back and dragging his hands down his face. He abruptly stands, his chair crashing to the floor as he backs away from the desk, the sudden movement making me nearly jump out of my seat. He glares at my screen with a snarl of absolute disgust, and without warning, he grabs the pencil holder and hurls it across the room. It hits the wall, and I jump again as the pencils and pens explode in every direction.

"Is *this* it? Is *this* the best that bitch could find? Is this what the next generation of best-selling authors will contribute? This mindless drivel?" He looks at me, disdain on his face. "*Is it?*"

"I... I..." Tears build in my eyes. He makes me feel so stupid and incapable, I'm beginning to actually despise him. "I don't know what else you want. I don't know what—"

"Is this what I can expect for the next *three* months?" he goes on as if I haven't said a thing. "Because I'll tell ya, Miranda, I don't know how much more of this I can take." He yanks the desk drawer open, and everything inside jostles. Fuming, he digs around before pulling out a stack of papers stapled together. "*Where* is the woman who wrote this? Huh?"

He tosses the papers on the desk. I glance at the title

page with my name typed across it.

He puts his hands to his head, throwing it back in the process. "Where is the *fucking* passion?"

My heart bangs against my ribs. He thinks I'm an idiot. He sees I can't do this. "I'm sorry. I just... you just... uh... I can..." I swallow. "You just make me nervous, and I'm trying really hard to write this the way you want me to. I just, you know, I have to go back and clean stuff up. I'm not a clean writer to begin with. I have to edit things, so it will be better once I go over it. I—" My vision blurs behind tears, my face heating with embarrassment because Edwin Mercer thinks I have no talent. And if he believes that, it must be true. "I... I..."

He looks sharply at me, his eyebrows burrowed, a sick look of pleasure washing over his face. "My dear, if you experienced even a second of my life's worst pain, it would crush you. Take this for what it is. And for the love of *fuck*, save me your tears." His tone drips with acid. "They're worthless."

Worthless. That is all I have ever been in my fucking life, and now he sees that. My chest tightens, and I fight the sob working its way up my throat. I quickly stand and run down the hallway to my room before slamming the door and locking it.

Leaning back against the cold wood, I break. I cry. Something that I thought would change my life—coming here to write with my goddam idol—has done nothing but prove to me I will never be anything. I'm useless. I'm worthless. I want to leave. I want out of here and away from his condescending ass. I grab my purse from the nightstand, dig out my cell phone, and pull up Janine's number. I press Call. Nothing. I hold the phone in the air as I walk around the room, pleading for those damn bars to light up. I stand on my tiptoes by the window, glaring out at that shed. But no. No service.

I don't want to go back out there and call her in front of him. I don't want him to see how defeated and dejected I am. I'll just stay in this room until he goes to bed if I must. Just as I'm putting my phone back inside my purse, I hear his boots tromping down the hallway. His door slams shut with such force a picture topples off the wall in my room.

I give it a few minutes, grab my phone, and slowly open the door. It's eerily quiet outside with just the soft tick-tock from the grandfather clock in the living room. The floorboards creak under my weight. I briefly freeze before continuing down the hallway, praying he doesn't come out of his room. I just don't want that conversation. At all.

The pens and pencils are still scattered across the living room, the chair knocked on its side. My foot lands on a stray pen, and I lose my footing, crashing into the console table behind the sofa. The sculpture of Atlas topples over, and I panic as I frantically reach to catch it, sighing when it lands in my hand and I'm able to set it back in its rightful place. I take a few deep breaths then hurry to the kitchen.

I'm nearly to the doorway when I hear a thud come from his room. Any moment now, I bet he'll come out yelling. The second I round the corner, I grab the kitchen phone. I quickly dial Janine's number, all the while staring down the hallway at the closed door of Edwin's room. She picks up on the second ring, and she sounds much too sweet to put up with an arrogant asshole like Edwin, but then again, I guess you'd need to be nice to handle him. She tells me it'll be an hour before she gets here.

I hang up, sneak back to my room, and pack my bags. *I am not a quitter. I am not worthless. Some things just aren't worth it...*

I'm almost to the front door with my suitcase when I stop dead in my tracks. I want one last look at that view, so I go stand in front of the window and wait. I should be taking in the scenery, the trees, the brilliant colors of the changing leaves, but I'm not. My gaze is aimed at that fucking shed. Why? Because every single time Edwin gets stuck, that's what he does. Stares at that shed as if it's going to give him all the answers. And right now, I'm stuck. Should I really leave?

After several minutes, I manage to pull my gaze from the shed to admire the scenery. And I take in the gorgeous backdrop of the Appalachian Mountains, trying to burn the image into my mind, because at the end of the day, no matter how big of a bastard Edwin is, it doesn't change how compelling his words are. He's still my idol, and *this* is what my idol looks at as he writes. And any time I drag up this image, I am, in a sense, looking through his eyes. If nothing else, I have that. I can steal this little piece of him, and he can never take it back, no matter how worthless I may be.

Sighing, I turn from the window and head toward the front of the cabin. I crack the door open, and a black Camaro sits in the drive.

A gust of wind kicks up, scattering dry leaves across the wooden porch as I make my way to the walkway. I can see Janine through the tinted windows, her dark hair piled on top of her head in a messy bun. She's smiling and waving from the driver's side. The trunk pops open, and she hops out then meets me at the side of the car to help me with my luggage.

"Thank you for coming to get me," I say before making my way to the back of the car.

She grabs my bag and places it in the trunk. Janine looks older than she sounds, older than you'd think someone who listens to the teenybopper crap on her stereo would be, but maybe the stress from working with him has aged her a bit. Maybe she's younger than she appears. Nonetheless, she's still pretty, her tiny waist accentuated by the tight sweater stretched across her massive breasts.

"No worries. Edwin's..." She grimaces. "He's hard to handle at times."

"Yeah, you could say that."

She laughs and slams the trunk. "He's been hard on

you, huh?"

"Hard is *one* way to put it."

Janine goes to the driver's side then stops. "Hey, I forgot about a conference call I had. Got half of my face on, then had to take the damn call, and, well, I can't very well go out in public like this. Would you mind driving? Otherwise, I'll just steer with one hand." She laughs, and I'm left standing with the passenger door open, staring at her.

I just met her. I don't really want to drive her car on roads I'm unfamiliar with, but I have a bad habit of not speaking up for myself, so I say, "Sure."

I walk around to the driver's side and climb in. We shut our doors at the same time.

Janine hauls her oversized Louis Vuitton bag into her lap and begins rummaging through it, pulling out a palette of eyeshadow and brushes. She glances up, a short snort leaving her nose. "Oh, well, look at Mr. Happy." Smiling, Janine leans down and waves.

I glance over my shoulder to see Edwin with his arms braced in the open doorway as he glares at the car. His face is red, his chest rising in ragged swells. I'm glad I'm in this car and not in that fucking cabin with him right now.

"He'll get over it, don't worry," she says, still waving as I put the car in drive and pull off.

———

A thick haze of smoke hangs in the air, and I fan it

away from my face as I glare at the man sitting across the bar, a cigarette dangling from his lips while his eyes are glued to a TV mounted on the wall.

"I thought you couldn't smoke inside anymore?" I ask through coughs.

"Yeah." Janine shrugs. "This place still lets you."

She's brought me to some run-down hole-in-the-wall bar. Dollar bills are tacked up all over the walls and ceiling. Half the barstools have tears in the leather seats, and the few tables scattered around the place are covered in that plastic red-and-white checkered tablecloth. An old white-haired man stumbles over to a jukebox in the corner, struggling to put his money in and stand at the same time.

"Ah, Darryl's done gone and got drunk before ten again," some random man shouts from the other end of the bar.

A few men cackle before returning to their conversations. Suddenly, some twangy country song blares over the sound system so loudly I can barely hear myself think. All the men hoot and holler. I just want to get the hell out of this shithole.

"You want a drink?"

I glance behind the bar and see a short, bald man leaning over the bar, winking at me.

"Uh, two shots of tequila," I say as I glance at Janine. She nods.

He nods and waddles off to pour the drinks.

"I really don't need anything." I shake my head. "I don't normally drink."

"Trust me, I didn't either until EA. He's a moody one."

The bartender places the shots on the counter, and Janine motions for me to take them.

"Drink up, sweetie." She smiles as I take the first shot back. "You gonna quit?"

"I can't handle him." I down the second tequila, coughing at the burn working its way down my throat.

"You have to learn *how* to handle him, that's the thing. He has mood swings." She shrugs. "Most really intelligent people do. When he gets pissed, just walk away. Give him a few minutes and he'll be fine."

"Uh-huh, but..." I arch a brow at her. "He's an asshole."

"Yeah, but he doesn't mean it. And besides, Miranda"—she places her hand on my knee, squeezing gently—"he's EA Mercer. The man could literally take a shit on a piece of paper and it would turn to gold. A few months of dealing with an asshole and you have a start to a writing career most people only dream of."

I inhale, thinking about the promise this opportunity could afford. How it could change my life. *That* could make me worth something. "I guess." I sigh.

"You have talent, honey. Trust me. Do you have any idea how many essays I had to read through? Yours"—she smiles—"was pure genius. You have a way with words, and

I'm not just saying that to blow smoke up your ass. He needs that. Edwin *needs* your voice."

Edwin Mercer needs *my* voice?

"Look, his last book—a lot of shitty reviews. Overall, three stars. That's not good. Have you read some of the reviews?"

Her ramblings about how Edwin doesn't take criticism well fade into the background as I think about what she's saying. It would be stupid to walk away, but to be honest, I don't know *if* I can handle him. He's volatile, and seeing as how I idolize him, any condescending remark he makes, well, it cuts my already battered and fragile ego to shreds.

A man settles in across the bar from us, leaning over the bar top and snapping to get the bartender's attention. He takes a quick survey of the bar, his eyes momentarily stopping on me. We hold eye contact for just a moment, but it's long enough for me to pick up on something all too familiar to me—sadness, a sense of being lost. In that brief look, we connect, and I know that he wishes he could be anywhere but here—that he's uncomfortable in his own skin.

"Think about him, how he is," Janine continues on, and I try to focus on her. "Do you know how hard those reviews have been for him? The amount of stress that man is under to have his next book receive good ratings? I'm afraid he's going to snap at any moment. Really, he's like a ticking time bomb and..."

My attention veers back to the man now tipping back a beer. His dark gray shirt clings to his arms, his chest. *Fuck.* His defined jaw is covered in stubble. He must feel me studying him because he nervously glances in my direction as he takes another slow sip from his bottle. I guarantee that man doesn't like attention. I bet it makes him nervous, and I'm almost positive I'm right because attention makes me nervous, so much so that I've debated on how I would actually handle it if I were to ever become a famous author. *A pseudonym. Never do interviews. Possibly even try to pass as a male—male authors tend to be taken more seriously anyway.*

The bartender says something to him, and he smiles. And *that* smile, with those dimples... well, it pulls me from my worrisome thoughts of how I'd handle fame. As if I need to worry about that anyway...

Janine clears her throat, and I glance back at her with my cheeks flaming. Arching her brow, she shakes her head. "He's in rare form lately because of it, I can promise you that. You, unfortunately, are getting the worst side of him I've seen in years. I promise, you just learn how to deal with him, and you will not regret it."

"Yeah... I don't know. I just need to..." My gaze drifts back to the guy at the bar, and I have to consciously force my attention back to Janine.

She turns on the stool to look behind her, shaking her

head and laughing before she faces me again. "Just *think* about it before you make a decision, Miranda." She stands, smoothing out her shirt as she grabs her purse from the back of the chair. "I'm going to go outside and make a call to the publisher. You stay here and..." She nods at the guy in gray. "Get yourself another drink, would you?"

"I really don't—"

"You really do. Unwind some. Take a little while to think it all over. I'll just be outside on the phone arguing for the next half hour anyway. You don't want to listen to that carnage, I promise." She gives the stranger at the end of the bar another fleeting glance, smiles at me, then heads to the door.

Fucking great. I watch her walk off, her hips swaying as she snakes between the men crowded around the bar. One wolf whistles, and she flips him the bird.

This entire ordeal is putting me so far out of my comfort zone it's ridiculous. I hate people. I hate crowds. I order two more shots. The bartender places them front of me, not even bothering to make eye contact before he trots off.

I grab one of the shots, rubbing my thumb over the curve of the glass. *Worthless...* I replay the disdain in Edwin's tone when he said that, and I cringe right before I down the shot, then the next one as I watch that stranger eye me from the other end of the bar. For whatever reason, I keep staring at him, pretending I can be that girl—a girl like Janine—a girl like I was when I met Edwin for coffee. I can be that girl who flirts with a guy and fucks him, knowing it'll never mean anything. I pretend to be the girl I would write about in my books because deep down inside, I know I'm not going to actually speak to him. Or maybe I will. Few people have ever intrigued me. And he does. That has to mean something...

CHAPTER SEVEN
Jackson

"Pain is a Gift"—Trade Wind

I didn't notice her when I first walked in, but by my sixth beer and second piss break, I'm wondering how the fuck I didn't. She has these big doe eyes that beg to be loved, flowing auburn hair—the kind you feel the insatiable desire to run your fingers through. She takes her shots like she's never taken one before and looks absolutely defeated. For a defeated guy like me, that's a welcome sight.

Not that I wish for everyone to feel as helpless as I do. I can promise you, I don't. It's just... misery loves company. That's a saying, right? I'm the kind of guy who only connects with people who can understand my pain. Even if it's a silent understanding, it's an understanding nonetheless. To be understood in this life, I mean to be truly understood, it's a gift. Not many people get to experience it.

And that understanding is about the only thing that could get me off of this damn stool. Everything in me tells me to go say something to her, but everything in me is also fighting the fear of failure, of rejection. I know she's looked at me. She's held my gaze. I'm not an idiot when it comes to understanding when someone may be interested in me. It's just the whole execution part that gets me.

She takes another shot, her face scrunching as it has with every shot before. It's quite endearing.

Before I even realize it, I'm standing, beer in hand, and walking toward her as though my legs are acting on their own free will. Her eyes never stray from mine. They're no longer projecting sadness but now carry an intoxicated twinkle.

I set down my beer and clear my throat. "Hi, I'm Jax. I don't mean to be a bother..." My heart is racing, temples thumping like rhythmic drums. I'm so nervous my palms actually start to sweat. I take a hard swallow and smile, flashing my teeth. Sometimes the smile is real, sometimes it's fake, but it *always* comes to the rescue when I need it to. It's my audible. "But I was wondering if I could buy you a drink?"

Smooth. Real smooth, big guy.

She coyly glances at the floor, grinning. And that smile is magnificent, the sight of it settling me a little. She puts out a hand and motions to the empty barstool.

"You can sit if you want," she says with a shrug.

I pull out the stool and take a seat, extending a hand to properly greet her. She obliges, placing her hand in mine, and I can't help but appreciate how her delicate hand is the polar opposite of my own—beat to shit and weathered from the years.

"I'm Miranda," she says then slips her bottom lip between her teeth.

"Nice to meet you, Miranda." I smile, releasing her hand before quickly taking a swig of my near-empty beer. I motion for the bartender.

"You as well, Jax." She averts her gaze to the floor then looks back at me, the timid smile still there.

There's an awkward moment of silence before the barkeep stops in front of us, and I place a quick order for a beer. As he walks away, I notice Miranda hasn't taken her eyes off me yet. She's got this drunken, glossy gaze. It's goofy but equally endearing.

"Sorry if I was staring too much." She leans her elbow on the bar, her eyes dropping to her lap. "Shit, what am I saying? But it's not like you didn't notice." She palms her forehead and shakes her head. "I don't know what... don't listen to me... shit, I'm drunk."

"If it's any consolation," I say, ignoring her last remark, "I was staring at you too. Hard not to. You're incredibly beautiful." The moment I say it, I wish I would've bit my tongue. *Am I coming on too strong?*

She looks at me, batting those beautiful eyes, her smile deepening and her cheeks flushing a deep crimson. "Thank you."

The bartender places the beer in front of me.

"I'm not gonna lie"—she lifts her bottle then nods toward the liquor shelf—"without this, I probably wouldn't be talking to you. I'm not a very social person."

"That makes two of us. My plan was three beers and then back to the house for a TV dinner and *Sons of Anarchy*. I surely didn't expect to meet anyone, but this is quite a nice surprise. It's been a long day."

"Oh, a long day, huh?" She shifts on the stool, tracing her finger over the worn bar top. "What do you do?"

"I'm a homicide detective. Been doing it a while now. It comes with its fair share of bullshit." I take a swig of beer and shrug. "But what can you do? Gotta pay the bills, right? What about you? What do you do?"

"Uh, well, I'm in school. Studying creative writing. Nothing too amazing or important." She clears her throat.

"Very nice. I'm quite the avid reader myself. Where do you go? UNC-Asheville? Warren Wilson?"

"Actually, I'm not from here. I am—well, *was*—only up here for a writing project, but I think that kinda fell through, so..." She takes a breath. "Well, I, uh... I should probably go." She nods as she hops off the stool. "Nice to meet you though."

For a moment, I'm left speechless. What I thought was a decent conversation has just abruptly ended for reasons beyond me. This is exactly why I don't approach women. This is just how shit goes for me. In the midst of my self-pity, I'm struck by the undeniable urge to be bold.

I pull a pen from my pocket, and after grabbing a napkin, I quickly jot down my name and number. I quickly stand and hold it out for her. "Well, take this at least. And if you find some time before you leave, call me or something." I stand holding that napkin out for what seems like eons before she takes it.

"Oh, sure," she says, a nervous smile twitching over her red lips. "Sure..." And with that, she turns and leaves.

I throw two fingers in the air and clear my throat. "Two more, Eddie. Jame-o."

CHAPTER EIGHT
Edwin

"Faces"—The Ratells

"You better have a real good goddamn explanation, Janine. And real fucking quick!" I bark into the phone, a blinding migraine sending surges of pain deep within my eye sockets and temples. The intense throbbing makes me wish I could take a fucking ax to my own neck.

"You said if she needed anything—anything at all—to take care of it. She called me... *scared*. And she wanted a ride to the city. She didn't feel safe there with your crazy ass. You never said anything about letting you in on our every move," she says with such a sense of calm it actually irritates me.

"Dammit, Janine, what if I'd felt inspired? What if I needed her to write? You know it can hit at any moment. You fucking *know* that. This is unacceptable."

"Listen to me... she may not even want to write with you anymore. You scared the shit out of her with that nasty temper. Throwing shit and belittling her."

She lets that sink in for a second, and to my surprise, it actually does. I *actually* feel a little guilty.

"You need to record yourself sometime when you get like that. It's frightening to—"

"Okay, okay, I get your point." I'm not one to be lectured. "Just bring her back. *Now.* I want to write."

"Are you not hearing me? She doesn't know if she wants to come back. She's thinking about going home. And I'll tell you the truth, I don't blame her. I've experienced you like that many times myself and—"

"*Enough,*" I say with a bite. I'm overcome with the intense desire to hurl the phone against the fucking wall, and if Janine were here, I'd bash her damn skull in with it. "I don't need to hear this shit. Just do what you must to get her back. Money, a massage, a fucking dildo for all I care. Just get her ass back here. I want to write."

"I've already talked to her a little bit tonight, and I will again first thing in the morning, but it's gonna take more than just me doing something here..." She takes a deep breath before continuing. "Just show her your good side. I've seen it. I know it's deep down there somewhere underneath all the arrogance and ego."

She snickers, and it makes me want to rip out her vocal chords, but... she's right. If I'm ever going to make something out of this book, if I'm ever going to get the weight of critics' bullshit off my shoulders, I need her.

"She's irreplaceable, Edwin. I'm the one that read

every story. Countless hours. Page after page after page. She's the one. She's the *only* one," she says with sincerity, and an awkward silence follows.

"Okay," I whisper, resigned in what I must do.

"She'll be just fine here with me tonight. I'll give you a call in the morning. Okay?"

"Okay," I repeat and hear a click on the other end of the line followed by a dial tone.

I keep the receiver against my ear for a moment longer, peering at nothing in particular, my thoughts wandering to places they shouldn't go. I finally hang up, grab my coat from the butcher block, and make my way to the front door.

It's time to relieve a little stress.

———

Janine's Camaro pulls up to the cabin at a quarter past noon, her convertible top down and some shitty Top 40 single blaring. To be a professional woman of forty years of age and listening to some Justin Bieber bullshit is just a travesty. What can I do? I hate the woman. I'd hack her to death if she weren't so damn good at her job. She's certainly dug her roots in nice and deep. Right about now though, I couldn't care less about her musical tastes. I'm just happy she's bringing Miranda back. *My* Miranda.

I didn't sleep well last night, tossing and turning and thinking about how I may have overreacted.

I open the door and step onto the porch just as Janine

hits the top step with Miranda's luggage. Miranda is a few steps behind her, and she's not looking at me, her eyes instead running loops across the gravel drive.

"Janine..." I barely look at her. My eyes are locked on Miranda, waiting for her to look up. "Miranda... good to see you both."

Miranda scoffs, and when she finally does look up, she smiles weakly. "You too."

It's barely audible. Her gaze once again falls to the ground, and she makes her way in after Janine. I take a moment on the porch, my eyes flitting over the rough edges of the mountains on the horizon as I give them time to get her stuff situated. My gaze trails down to my pine-tree-riddled property, thick aging pines that stand as a border to everything... and everyone.

Taking one last deep breath of the rich country air, I head inside to meet them. They're talking in hushed tones in the office. Of course, the conversation quickly changes to normal volumes when I approach. As if I don't know they were discussing me.

"Janine, if you wouldn't mind, I'd like to speak with Miranda. If that's okay with you."

Janine glances at Miranda, a look of concern on her face that makes my fucking blood boil, and Miranda just nods.

"Okay, well, Miranda, it was so nice getting to know you a little better." She takes Miranda in a hug and holds her for a few moments before pulling back, her hands still holding each of her fragile little arms. "If you need anything, anything at all, I'm a phone call away." She lets go and walks right past me to the front door, her finger up and curling for me to follow.

I reluctantly do and meet her just outside the front door. She shuts it just as a cold breeze sweeps around the corner of the house.

"Edwin..." she starts. I fight the urge to head back in and slam the door in her face. "You gotta take it a little easier on her. She hasn't written seven best sellers—"

"Eight," I interrupt.

She rolls her eyes, and I envision her head clamped in a vice as I turn the handle ever so slowly, watching her eyes bulge out from their sockets.

"Yeah, okay, eight. Eight best sellers. She's not in her thirties. She's a young woman still figuring herself out. I've been married to three different cheating assholes. I ate shit for five years with each of them so that I could take them for everything they were worth when it was all said and done. And I did just that. Me"—she points at her chest—"I can handle your shit. But give her a break, okay? She's... I don't know... fragile."

"I will do that. I've already planned on it. Just know, Janine, you've been with me a long time now, and I like your work, I do, but if you ever talk to me like that again, I'll fire your ass." I glare at her, maintaining eye contact for

STEVIE J. COLE & BT URRUELA

a moment before turning to open the door.

"Edwin, my dear, if I had a dollar for every time you said you'd fire me or did in fact 'fire me,' I wouldn't even have to work for you anymore." She laughs, making her way to the Camaro, and before I can respond, she hops in and starts it up. Bieber's preteen vocals once again tarnish the beautiful country silence.

I shake my head, flicking her off before closing the door to three long honks of her horn.

Miranda is standing in the office when I come in the house, her gaze fixated out the bay window. She turns her head just slightly when the floorboards creak beneath my feet, and the light hits her face just right. So right that it stops me dead in my tracks. I take her in. The soft, delicate look of her skin, pale—not in a sickly way, but like porcelain, rich and alluring. A living muse. She turns completely now, a wrinkle of confusion in her brow.

"Sorry, I don't mean to stare. It's just... in that light... you truly inspire."

She smiles politely but instinctively looks at her feet.

I take a few steps forward, drawing her eyes again. "Though I will stow the urge to write away for a bit. I have something for you."

I walk past her, my arm brushing hers, and a sudden, smoldering desire takes hold deep in my gut. I fight the urge to take her into my arms and destroy her—with my lips and my cock—and proceed to the desk as planned instead.

I pull a small duffel bag from beneath it and place it on top, smiling at her as I do. She raises an eyebrow in confusion but with a look of intrigue at least.

"I have a present for you..." I motion to the duffel bag then walk to the closet across the room. After opening it, I pull out a long, bulky bag housing a folded up tent and set it against the wall.

This draws even more confusion from Miranda, her brow furrowing and eyes narrowing. I can't help but smile at the thought of knowing something she doesn't. I like having secrets... big ones *and* small.

"Two presents, I guess," I say, making my way back to her.

"I'm so confused," she mutters, her eyes shifting from the duffel bag to the tent.

"You won't be for long, but before I go into your first gift, I, um..." My eyes drift from hers. I fucking hate apologies. Janine's annoying, Jersey-tainted voice rings in my ears, and that alone makes me cringe. But I have a job to do and a book to write. If I'm to ensure that happens, this is where it starts. "I just want to tell you how sorry I am. My actions... I... I was out of line. I know you're new to this industry and all, but I can't tell you what these deadlines can do to a person. They loom over you, breathing down your neck, suffocating you..." My voice trails involuntarily as my gaze fixes out the window, across the pines. "She's a ruthless, daunting little bitch. And she's waiting for your ass whether you like it or not."

Looking back over, I see that I have all of her attention now. Her eyes are full of understanding, and she nods slowly.

"I get it." She puts a hand to her mouth and shakes her head. *So cute, my little Miranda.* "I mean, I don't necessarily *get it*, not yet, but I can see how it could be horrible."

"It is. And I don't know what Janine told you—I'm sure it was more than I could even stomach knowing—but I have the tendency to act on impulse. At times, to a fault." I look her in the eyes and impulsively take her hand in both of mine. She looks startled, but I continue holding it regardless as I paint the perfect look of sincerity onto my face. "I just want you to know it'll never happen again. You're a very talented writer, truly."

I give her hand a good squeeze then release it, turning my attention to the duffel bag. I unzip it and begin pulling out its contents: noise-canceling headphones, a mini stop sign, and a laptop still in its box. I toss the bag aside, and my eyes meet hers, a mischievous little smile on my face. A look of total bewilderment on hers.

"I feel like shit about how I treated you, and I want to take the appropriate measures to see that it doesn't happen again. So I'd like to make a deal. How's that sound?" Another timid smile. Soft, unassuming eyes.

"I, uh, I appreciate the apology. I'm sure it's different

working with someone when you're used to working alone." She curiously glances at the items on the desk then back at the tent. "But... um, can you explain to me what all this stuff is for?"

I laugh, understanding how odd this all must look. I reach first for the stop sign, holding it up by its thin wood handle, waving it and smiling. "So at UNC, in my earlier creative writing classes, I had this crazy professor, Tony Harris. He was the first real writing inspiration I had. He had some rather peculiar teaching habits." I lift the stop sign once more then set it back on the desk. "One of them involved these stupid little stop signs. Any time peer-to-peer writing criticism went from productive to personal, you'd hold up the sign. So in this circumstance, if you think I'm out of line, if I'm too harsh or too critical..." I point at the sign and shrug. "Just shove that shit in my face."

She laughs. "Okay. And"—she points back at the desk—"the headphones?"

"See, that's stage two. If the stop sign doesn't work, just throw on these bad boys. I have a pair I travel with, and trust me, my griping will go undetected." I set my hand against the laptop, scanning her face, trying my best to read her. I'm not used to having to do this, having to win someone over. It's unnerving and nauseating. "The laptop is for you. It's stage three. I know you already have one, but I noticed it's not in the, um, best condition..." I fight a laugh back as the thought of her dreadful laptop crosses my mind.

"I had Janine load this one up with a writing program that's linked to our computers in here. Again, top of the line. If you need to get away, maybe go outside and write, or in your room or whatever, just take that with you." I scan the items on the desk, my fingers nervously picking at my arm. "I want this to work. I *need* this to work." I swallow hard. My stomach knots. "And I'll do what I have to to make sure that happens."

Her eyes narrow on me, as though she's scrutinizing me for a brief moment, before she drags in a breath. "I think it will all work out, and I really do appreciate the laptop..." Her voice drifts off, and we stand in awkward silence for a moment. "So what the hell is that thing for?" She points toward the corner of the room.

I laugh, glancing back at the tent leaning against the wall. I look back at Miranda, undeniably taken by her cute look of intrigue. "I know how I can get. I can only imagine what that's like for someone who's just met me. I've thought a lot about it..." My eyes scan the floor. *Genuine remorse? What the fuck is this?* "Anyways, I'm going to pitch that tent out back and go on a little three-day 'writing retreat.' I'll give you free rein of the house and won't bother you at all. I have a fire pit down there, food already set up in coolers, and an outdoor shower behind the shed. Consider it a three-day vacation from my miserable ass."

Her brow wrinkles, and she shakes her head. "Edwin, that's really unnecessary. It's your house. The apology..."

Her eyes wander to the items on the desk. "All this... it's more than enough."

I put up a hand, shaking my head. "I'm afraid I have to insist. I do this sort of thing all the time. It allows me to clear my head... connect with the earth. I always come out completely inspired. Trust me when I say I have more camping equipment than the fucking army. I'll be fine regardless. You just make yourself comfortable up here."

She blankly stares at me for a moment, biting her bottom lip. "Well..." She sighs as her eyes drift from me to the tent and back. "I guess whatever helps you to feel inspired."

I walk to the closet and grab the tent, throwing the strap over my shoulder. As I pass Miranda, I glance at her, a telling smile on my face. "By the way, be up and ready by nine tomorrow. Janine will be by to grab you." I face forward and continue out of the office. Without turning around, I continue, "I've got a full spa day scheduled for you in Asheville: massage, facial, the works. Enjoy!"

With that, I open the front door and make my way out, hoping to hell my hooks have started to dig in.

———

The fire crackles loudly in the still night air. Its warmth makes the forty-degree temperature irrelevant. Seated in a rocker just in front of the tent, I hold my hands to the fire. My eyes scan the cabin windows, waiting impatiently for the lights to turn out. I glance at my watch.

Eleven o'clock. She should be asleep at any point now, knowing she has the spa in the morning. My nervous rocking creates a chorus of crunching leaves beneath my chair. The sound worms its way into my brain, but I can't stop rocking. I *will* the lights to turn off. But they don't.

Just as the tension begins to threaten my sanity, the lights *do* go out, and the jolt of adrenaline that surges through my body is similar to jumping out of an airplane for the first time—a relentless, nerve-shattering strike of equal parts panic and pleasure.

Standing from the rocker, I scan the windows as I back up to the tent. I make my way around the tent and to the shed directly behind it. Retrieving the key from my pocket, I unlock the bottom padlock then put in the combination to the top lock. The wind picks up, sending a shiver down my spine. There's something odd about being here and doing this with someone not a hundred yards away. I take one last glance around the tent toward the windows. The lights are still off. All is quiet and calm.

I open the door slowly, and I'm met immediately with the sound of muffled sobbing. I step into the shed, closing the door behind me, and I flip on the lights.

The whore's eyes bat in reaction to the flood of fluorescent light since it's been a day since she was last exposed to it. Her naked body squirms beneath the restraints but to no real effect. Her breathing picks up, pushing and pulling the duct tape over her mouth—in, out, in, out—with each wrangled breath. When her eyes finally adjust and they fixate on me with a look of absolute terror, the strike of adrenaline hits me again, racing from limb to limb like electricity.

It doesn't go away this time though. No, it spikes in intensity with each step I take toward her, with each time she flinches from my every movement. Inspiration will come... and it will come through pain. It will come through bloodshed.

I run a gloved finger slowly up the length of her body, tsking as I shake my head from side to side. "No, no, no, my dear. There's no use in crying." I stop at her nipple and hover my finger there for a moment before marking a pretend X over both of them. "Your fate has been decided. It was written long ago." I settle a hand against her throat and squeeze, just enough to drive the point home. I lean in, my lips against her ear, and whisper, "I am the executioner... and tonight—tonight, your number's been drawn."

CHAPTER NINE
Miranda

"Dark in My Imagination" – of Verona

I can't sleep. Every noise, every creak and pop in this house leaves me unnerved.

Being in a stranger's house while he's camped out in his backyard—a stranger who isn't exactly that because for years you've all but worshipped him—is an odd feeling. A gust of wind howls around the corner of the house. The bare branches of the tree outside my window scratch against the pane. That noise makes me cringe.

I stare at the ceiling, watching the shadows from the limbs dance across it. There is no way I'm finding sleep any time soon. I roll onto my side and turn on the lamp before grabbing the strap of my satchel and hauling it up onto the bed. I dig through, looking for my plot book, but instead, I pull out *Echoes of the Fall*. This is one of my favorites of Edwin's books. My fingers slowly trace over his name. EA Mercer.

And isn't this something? Here I—little Miranda

Cross—sit, snuggled down in his guest room bed, in the very house these words were written. I know what he looks like when he's pissed, when he smiles. I know what he smells like. I know things so many of his fucking readers would love to know, and something about holding this book in this very room is exhilarating.

I turn to the first chapter, my eyes poring over his words.

Her eyes bead with tears—worthless tears—as I wrap the duct tape around her pretty mouth. I'm not exactly sure why I cover their mouths like this. It's not like anyone would hear her pitiful screams coming from this cabin in the middle of the woods—

And my attention darts from the book to the window, all too aware of where I am right now. Chills splinter up my spine. I don't scare easily. In fact, for the most part, I thrive on fear.

"Don't be ridiculous," I whisper to myself. "You've written some fucked up shit before."

And I have. I wrote about stabbing Margaret Stanley, and I loved every word I put on that paper, but I didn't actually kill her. I *wouldn't* kill her. My gaze veers back to the window, to the faint glow of the bonfire bouncing off the trees. He's peculiar... but aren't we all? Aren't we all quirky and strange? I know damn well my penchant for dark stories comes from the abuse, from the demons I keep hidden deep inside me. It's an outlet for my shame and anger over the fucked up hand life dealt me.

I attempt to read some more, but for the first time in my life, I can't stomach his words. And it's not because they aren't beautiful; it's because my idol is human. I understand that he may very well have some dark, twisted past that parallels mine. And that leaves me unsettled. Why? Because his books were my escape, a haven if you will. They were fiction that let me avoid the shit that was my life, and due to my overactive imagination—because that's what it is, my mind running wild in an effort to rob me of sleep—I fear that maybe he isn't the person I always dreamed he was.

And with that thought, I turn off the lamp and settle beneath the sheets, wondering what kind of demons he's hiding. Because that is one thing all humans have in common—we all have some type of demon riding our backs. Some are just far worse than others.

———

I stare out of the windshield, my hands gripping the steering wheel. Janine went to have drinks while I was at the spa. One too many, she said as she tossed me her keys. I don't like driving her car. The gas pedal is too sensitive, the steering wheel too tight. She's put the radio on some pop station. Each song blaring through the speakers is more annoying than the last, and she's singing along. When she turns the volume down, I'm thankful, but I know that's my cue to glance at her.

"How can you look *that* tired after a day at the spa?" Janine asks.

I shrug. "Didn't sleep well, I guess." And I didn't. I barely slept last night.

"Oh." She points out of the window. "Turn in there. I'm starved."

I put the blinker on and check the rearview before switching to the far right hand lane.

"So you said EA was camping out?" She laughs. "Him and his ways to find inspiration. Give me cable and a bottle of cab sav any day. That's plenty inspiration. Who needs dirt and the elements?"

I laugh, not because I find it funny but because I know that's how she meant it. "Yeah, I guess everyone has their thing."

"Like I said, he's a nice guy, just a little quirky."

"Yeah, well." I sigh. "The fact that he apologized speaks volumes."

"That it does. All these years and I think I've gotten one 'I'm sorry' that sounded more like a sneeze and a fart than anything."

I pull in between two pickup trucks, the bed of one filled with wire cages housing chickens.

"A burger okay? This place has the *best* burgers," she says, not really waiting on a response as she opens the car door and hops out.

"Yeah, fine." I'm speaking to myself because Janine's

already heading toward the entrance of the tiny restaurant. I shut the door, lock the car, and jog to catch up with her.

"Don't let the looks of it scare you," she throws over her shoulder. "And don't look at the health rating either."

The tiny bell hung above the entrance jingles as a group of men dressed in blue coveralls open the door to the diner. They hold it for us, and we skirt around them. The thick smell of grease slaps me in the face the second we step inside, and my nose crinkles. I follow Janine to the counter and take a seat on one of the red stools.

A frazzled-looking waitress is sorting silverware behind the counter. She looks up and grins, revealing a gap-toothed smile. "Hey there, baby doll. Give me just a second, and I'll be right with ya."

Janine smiles and hands me a menu. "The Classic is the best, and the Coke floats here..." Her eyes roll back in her head, and she bites her lip. "They are *amazing*."

I skim over the menu, every so often eyeing the grill that looks as though it hasn't been cleaned in months. Janine rambles on and on about how good the food is, but I don't really believe her. And I definitely don't look for that little framed piece of paper with the health rating on it either.

After the waitress takes our order, Janine turns her chair toward me and smiles. "So that guy the other night, the one at the bar..."

I stare blankly at her. "Yeah?"

"You gonna meet up with him at any point?"

"What? No."

A group of men sitting across the counter from us are staring and whispering. *Damn perverts.*

"Why the hell not? Did you not get a good enough look at him?" She tosses her menu on the counter. "His muscles, his face—a man like *that* would ruin you."

"Uh, I'm not really... you know. I just..."

The waitress sets my soda in front of me, and I take the opportunity to glance away from Janine's look of utter shock. This entire socializing bullshit is not my forte.

"Miranda?"

I slowly turn to look at her. "Yep?"

"Any normal woman would climb that man like a tree. I mean, hell, what, are you a virgin or a Jehovah's Witness? Are you into girls or something?"

"No." I take another sip of my drink, staring at the piece of overly processed meat sizzling on the griddle.

"Okay, so I don't understand the problem here. He—" She places her hand on my shoulder and spins my chair to face her. "What was his name?"

"Jax."

"Sexy name." She smiles. "So *Jax* was obviously interested. You were interested. I mean, hell, you two were basically eye-fucking each other."

Covering my mouth, I choke on my drink. To be so crude, she sure as hell looks put together. "I'm not really a people person."

Janine rolls her eyes. "Yeah, yeah. I haven't met an author yet who is a 'people person.' Did you give him your number?"

"Hell no... he gave me his."

She arches one of her perfectly sculpted brows. "Interesting."

"What's interesting about that?"

"That he gave you his number instead of asking for yours." She shrugs. "I like to analyze people, figure out what makes them tick. That's the only reason I work well—huh, as well as one person can work—with EA. You have to learn what drives someone, you know, and the fact that he gave you *his* number, well, he put the damn ball in your court..." She smirks before lifting her drink to her lips. "Life is about experiences, Miranda. Do something that takes you out of your comfort zone."

"Oh." I laugh. "I assure you this entire ordeal with Edwin"—I wave my hand—"way, *way* out of my comfort zone."

Shooting a disapproving look at me, she shakes her head. "Just call the damn man, would you? One call. Ask him to have coffee with you or something." She turns back to the counter just as the waitress sets a plate filled with soggy fries and a gigantic burger in front of her. "Coffee and a quick fuck, is that too much for a woman to ask for?"

Easy enough for her to say. Not in a million-fucking-years would I call him. No matter how badly I may want to.

CHAPTER TEN
Jackson

"People Are Strange"—Goodbye Nova

"You're fucking sick, man. I'm telling ya. A fuckin midget? Really?" Tommy asks, scratching his slightly balding head.

"A hot one? Yeah, what's there not to get here, man? You can spin them. Carry them around. There are all kinds of benefits," I say, my eyes counting the cracks in the sidewalk, my brain anywhere but engaged in this ridiculous conversation. If I had known my comment after passing a shop with a midget stripper billfold in the window would've led to this conversation, I would've kept my mouth shut.

A migraine is rocking my skull right now, and my aviators do little to keep the noon sun from making matters worse. Nightmares kept me up most of the night. The kind that make you feel like you're right there in it. Living and breathing the nightmare, fighting to get out. I sat up and drank and stared blankly at some shitty TV rerun until the sun came through the shades.

Cruising Tenth Street for prostitutes with my chatty partner is not how I want to spend my day.

"You just wanna see them tiny carnie hands around your junk so it makes you feel like I do every day." He laughs heartily, pulling at his junk then putting both hands to his gut. With each bit of laughter, jolts of pain tear through my brain.

"Fuck, Tommy, can you keep it down? I'm fucking dying over here."

"Yeah, you don't look so good. Long night?" he asks, a pep in his step that makes me hate his ass right about now.

"Yeah."

"Nightmares and shit again?"

"Don't you know it," I say with a bland tone as I make the turn down an alley peppered with half-clothed prostitutes.

A few of them scatter, trying their best to act inconspicuous. One drops what's obviously a joint and follows them.

"C'mon now, ladies. No one's in trouble here. We just wanna talk," Tommy calls.

"Ain't nobody wanna talk to you, pig!" one of them yells, leaning nonchalantly against the brick wall. Her bleached-blond hair is in pigtails, and a tiny black mini skirt hugs her tight ass.

Tommy just laughs as we approach her. He looks over

STEVIE J. COLE & BT URRUELA

at me. "Well, ain't she sweet, partner?" He looks back over at her. "You on your period or something, sweetheart?"

She flips us both the bird before slinking around the corner, disappearing into some old shop.

"They're not gonna talk to us," I say as I turn toward Tommy, whose attention has been drawn to the hot dog stand on the corner.

"Partner..." he says without looking. "Fucking hot dog time."

I follow him as he's guided by his gut to the rickety little cart with a white-and-yellow striped umbrella. The man behind the cart is busy slopping wet hot dogs onto buns. He opens one of the containers, and the smell of chili wafts up in a cloud of steam.

"He's picking up speed. Killing faster than he used to." I mumble more to myself than to Tommy as he places his order.

"He's agitated, all right." He hands a wad of cash to the vendor before taking the hot dog and immediately burying it inside his mouth. "Did you see the mouth on that cunt..." He shakes his head, his mouth full of food. "I would have throttled that one *real* good."

I pass him a look of complete disgust, but it goes unnoticed. "Finish. Chewing. Please."

But he just laughs, bits of hot dog escaping his mouth. That's about the time I decide to walk away. I hear him shuffling behind me as I cross the street, and I roll my eyes as he grunts through the last of the hot dog. He catches up, wiping grease from his face with his suit jacket, just as my phone rings.

I pull it from my pocket and answer the call. "Hello?"

"Um, is this, uh, Jax?" a familiar voice asks.

"This is him. May I ask who's calling?"

There's a pause before the woman clears her throat. "Miranda. I, uh... met you in that bar the other night..."

Now I'm left without words. I know exactly who she is, though I didn't spend nearly enough time with her, because she hasn't left my mind in the day since I met her. I was hoping she'd call, but I surely wasn't expecting it.

"Miranda? Yes, of course. Sorry, I wasn't really sure if you'd call or not." I swallow hard, fighting back the nerves. "I'm glad you did though."

"Yeah, I don't really do stuff like this and I—" There's a rustle over the line, and I can make out her whispering to someone. "Fine, Janine," Miranda says with a groan. "Look, I'm in Asheville. Do you want to have coffee or something?"

Without a second's thought, I respond, "Off Fletcher and Richter Streets. There's a little coffee joint down there. It's right by the baseball stadium. Would that work?"

"Yeah. Sure. Um, what time?"

"I gotta drop my partner off at the station. Give me fifteen?" I ask, pushing Tommy away as he's started eavesdropping.

"Yep. See you there."

"I look forward to it," I say before hanging up. Without my even realizing it's happened, a shit-eating grin has taken up my face.

"What the fuck was that?" Tommy asks, a suspicious look in his eyes.

"Don't you worry about it, fucker. C'mon, let's go."

———

She's already in the diner when I walk in, seated at the counter with her back to the door and a coffee in her hands. For a fleeting moment, I think about turning around and hitting the liquor store, maybe grabbing some last-minute liquid courage. Instead, I muster up the natural stuff and work my way toward her. When I tap on her shoulder, her head turns.

"Hey, Miranda, sorry I'm a little late. Traffic here can be a pain."

She smiles. "It's fine."

I notice her foot bobbing up and down, a lip between her teeth. She looks more settled today, more relaxed, like whatever was bothering her the other day has been lifted. I like that a lot. She was beautiful when she was sad, but with just a little more light in her eyes, it takes my best not to be a bumbling asshole.

When I realize that I've been standing entirely too long, I put up a palm and motion to the stool beside her. "Mind if I take a seat?"

"Nope." She smiles—just barely—nodding at the stool, and I sit before the nerves take my legs completely out from under me.

I motion to the waitress for a coffee of my own then redirect my attention to Miranda, though her rich hazel eyes are scanning the countertop.

"So..." Words are lost to me. I haven't been on a date, or whatever the hell this is, for a long time. And certainly not sober. I've almost forgotten how the fuck to do it. *Fucking say something, man!* "I gotta say, you were the last person I was expecting on the other end of that call. And you even ignored the three-day rule. *Nice!*" I say as playfully as I can, though I probably come off sounding more like a total jackass.

She shrugs. "Yeah... something like that." She brings the coffee cup to her lips, her gaze dropping to the grease-stained floor.

She's so short with me that I can't tell if she's not into me or just quiet. I remind myself that she probably wouldn't have called if it were the former as my sweaty hands fumble with a fresh cup of coffee.

"How much longer do you have here?" I ask.

Her eyes lift back to mine. "A few weeks. But, um, I'm not actually staying here, you know, in Asheville."

"Oh, that's right. So where about are you? I've lived here in North Carolina my whole life."

"In the middle of East-Budda-Fuck up in the

mountains. About fifty miles outside of town, I guess. Some place called Devil's Hatchet. Fitting place for an author, huh?"

My eyes go wide, the coffee mug settling back on the counter. There's only one author anyone knows up in those mountains, and he happens to be one of my favorites. "Wait a second. EA Mercer lives up that way. And you said you were here for writing research. So..."

She cracks a grin. "You know the name?"

I nod. "Who doesn't? The guy is a genius. Detective Bryce Hernandez from his *Bloodlust* series is the reason I became a cop."

"No kidding? I love the gruesome way he describes those murder scenes..." She shudders a little. "Unbelievable."

"I can definitely appreciate his ability to make you feel like you're right there in the story, but it's the character development that I've always loved the most. He has the most ruthless villains. Tragic, unapologetic heroes. It's the best."

"I love the tragic heroes. Fuck all that flowery bullshit other people write. That's not life. His stuff is raw and gritty and just..." She gets lost in her words and bites her lip, her eyes locking with mine.

I laugh, knowing exactly what she's talking about and appreciating the commonality. "Let me tell ya... there's only one other big-time author anywhere close to here, and his name is Nicholas Sparks." Her face wrinkles with disdain, and I grin. "So I know all about that flowery crap. No fucking thanks."

She laughs, and fuck, she's adorable when she does. "Have you ever met him?"

"No, never have. Actually, that's the thing. No one's really met him. The stories around Asheville about EA Mercer are abundant, though they're all just hearsay. No one's ever really seen the guy...kind of a hermit, I guess." I laugh. "So wait, you said you're here for writing research... tell me you're not trying to meet the guy. I'm not trying to discourage you here, but he's literally a ghost. I mean, he has an assistant who does everything for him, right down to his grocery shopping, and from what I've heard, all she does is bitch about what an asshole her boss is."

"Oh, well"—she arches a brow—"while he *is* a literary genius, he *absolutely* has his moments where he's a big-time dick." She shakes her head. "He means well, I think, just has a very short fuse."

My body stiffens and eyebrows rise. *"No way.* You're fucking with me, right?"

"What? That he's a huge dick? No." She takes a sip of her coffee, smiling around the cup rim.

"No, the fact that you actually *know* he's a huge dick. How? Spill."

Her eyes drop to her lap, and she fidgets with a loose piece of thread on her shirt. "I, uh... I'm doing this book with him. I mean, it's not really a—it's more of a writing project. So anyway, he had me come up to his cabin to work on it with him, and well, he can just be an asshole sometimes." She glances at me, a nervous grin inching across her lips. "So, yeah..."

I glance from side to side and twist around to scan behind me before looking back at her. "Am I on *Punk'd* right now or something? You said you're still in school, didn't you? And he's EA Mercer. Did you win some kind of author lottery?"

Her cheeks flush, and she shrugs. "Kinda. I won some contest he held to find a co-author." An uneasy laugh bubbles from her throat, then she swallows hard. "Crazy, huh?"

I put my head in my hands and run my fingers through my hair. "Consider my mind blown. *Very* impressive. You must be one hell of a writer."

Now her cheeks are full-on red. "I'm just... sick in the head enough for him, maybe?"

"Well, the cat is out of the bag. I'm going to go ahead and apologize ahead of time if this ever dominates future conversations. Just give me a swift kick to the shin or something to reset me."

"It's fine. And I'm not kicking you."

"So I'm going to assume, by that response, that there will, in fact, be future conversations?" I smile, though I can feel my face flush with nervousness. I've never been confused for being smooth. That's just not who I am.

"I mean"—she swallows—"sure."

My gaze fixes on the tiled wall. I'm unable to read this woman whatsoever. I finish my coffee, and without turning to her, I say, "I like the enthusiasm." I smile, the cup still held to my lips.

"I'm not one to get overly excited about anything... but I do like talking to you, and I don't like most people, so there's that."

"Oh yeah, you either?" I say, setting the cup down, a devious smile stretching across my face.

"Nope. People are assholes."

"I spent three years in the army. Two of them were spent fighting against the most vile pieces of shit this world has to offer." My eyes drift to hers. "It takes the optimism right out of a man. When it comes to humanity at least. I guess that's why I became a cop." I lean in just a bit, smile, and shrug. "Well, that and EA Mercer."

"Thank you for your service," she blurts then inhales an uneven breath. I get the feeling she's never exactly certain when to say something or how to say it.

That comment though—I can't help but internally cringe. Sometimes I feel that by talking about my service, I'm invoking some sort of appreciation. I'm not. I'm just talking about me, and I know she likely means her thank you, but I still can't help but feel it's most often said because it's the *only* thing to say.

"Thanks," I say, my voice unsteady. "It was honestly my pleasure. It's what made me the man I am today." My eyes stray to the clock on the wall and then back to her. "The good, the bad, the ugly. I'm a better man for it."

A long awkward moment passes between us that makes me both uncomfortable and a bit more attracted to her. She's as socially dysfunctional as I am. I can only look at her and weakly smile.

"Can I mention I'm not the best in these types of situations?" I say. "If I'm being perfectly honest—which hell, after *that* awkward little moment of silence, why the hell not?—I haven't been on a date, or in a situation like this, in a while. A *long* while." I can feel heat radiating throughout my body. Dealing with bullets and bombs—no problem. Talking to a woman without the assistance of alcohol and I'm in fucking full panic mode. "So I tend to have a little word vomit from time to time. You'll just have to bear with me."

She laughs, tossing her head back a little, her auburn hair falling down her back. "Trust me, Jax, I suck at conversation in general, much less with a guy like you..." Her eyes widen. "I mean, you know a guy. Just a guy, not like there's anything, uh..." Her gaze drops to my lap, and she flinches. "Yeah... so. How about you just don't worry about my word vomit and I won't worry about yours?"

I laugh, impressed by her candor. "I like the sound of that." My eyes drift again to the clock. The time reads five minutes past when I told Tommy I'd be back, and I can already hear his shit-talking. I pull out my wallet and toss a ten on the counter before stowing my wallet away. "I've gotta get back to work. But I'd like to see you again. I need you to let me know when I can make that happen."

"Okay. Sure."

I can only shake my head and laugh as I stand from the stool. "You and that 'sure.'" I make my way to the door and hold it open for her as she stands from her own stool.

"Fine." She grins as she heads toward me. "I'd *love* to see you again. I'd be *ecstatic*."

Pointing at her as she passes through the doorway, I raise my eyebrows. "*That's* more like it."

Without another word, she turns and makes her way down the sidewalk in the opposite direction of my cruiser. I can't help but feel both confused and intrigued. She doesn't say a word, but I can see a little pep in her step. *Maybe I put that there.*

I cup a hand to my mouth. "So you'll call me then?" I say with a wide grin.

"Sure," she responds.

CHAPTER ELEVEN
Miranda

"Devil Side" - Foxes

Janine's singing along to the radio. And she is as tone-deaf as they come. I drive her car along the twisted road through the thick woods. We top a small hill, and Edwin's cabin appears in the distance—along with that shed and his tent set up between it and the house.

Janine laughs. "He *actually* set up a tent." She shakes her head. "EA, the survivalist."

"Yeah, and let me tell you, I feel weird staying in his house alone."

"Don't." The car rolls to a stop in front of the walkway that leads to the porch. "He'll only stay out there a few days, and when he comes back in, you'll be praying to the baby Lord Jesus for him to go back out there." She laughs at herself. "I promise."

I stare at the tent, my gaze drifting instinctively toward the shed.

"Well"—she pats my shoulder—"you call me if you

need anything, alright?"

"Yep." I feign a smile as I open the driver's door and gracelessly clamber out of her sports car. "Thanks again."

"Don't thank me." She's already climbed out of the passenger's side, and her eyes are set on the tent. "Thank him. That spa's not cheap."

My eyes remain trained on his tent, wondering if he's out there or in that shed or gone. The wooden porch steps creak beneath my weight. A crow in a nearby oak caws, its wings fluttering as it takes flight, and I suddenly realize how eerily quiet it is out here. How alone we are. So far away no one would hear me screaming—*stop it, Miranda. Stop being so ridiculous.*

The door's still unlocked, and it swings open to the empty living room. The late evening sun pours in from the bay window, casting a warm light over the elk head mounted on the fireplace.

What do I do? This is honestly the most awkward situation I have ever found myself in—and for me, that says a lot. He said to make myself at home, but really, who in the hell could do that? The only place I feel somewhat comfortable is my room, and I think that's because I can shut the door and lock it... so that is exactly where I go.

I drag out my new laptop, boot it up, and open the writing program Edwin mentioned. For half an hour, I read over what we've written, surprised at how well our writing styles complement one another. To be honest, I'm not sure who wrote what; it's almost as if we have the same voice. I guess that's the perk of obsessing over and dissecting the way someone writes.

I come to the abrupt end of my last chapter, and my fingers hover over the keys, my brain scrambling to get into the right headspace. *She's in the room. All the lights are out due to the blizzard. He's somewhere in the house... what would I do if it were me?*

Finally finding the words, I type.

She sits, waiting, her heart in her throat, knowing that at any moment, she may draw her last breath because she's finally realized he's utterly mad. Although his demeanor appears calm, she knows that deep down inside, a constant bloodlust drives his next breath. He's a monster, not even sure of who he really is himself...

A floorboard outside of the door creaks, and I stop typing. I sit in the middle of the bed, staring at the door, waiting to see if the knob twists. My pulse clangs in my temples, adrenaline buzzing down my arms to my fingertips. Seconds tick by, but there is no movement, so I go back to my writing. I stare at the blinking cursor... and all the thoughts, the words, they're now nothing but a jumbled mess.

Groaning, I shove the laptop away and shake my head in disgust. I stand and make my way to the window, pull back the curtain, and peer out at Edwin's tent. Not once has he come inside. He's just been out there "finding his inspiration." I have to laugh at it because otherwise, it unnerves me. And the longer I look out at the scenery—that tent billowing in the breeze, that shed—my imagination runs wild. What if *he's* really crazy? What if he's out there roasting human flesh over that open fire at night? What if...

"Miranda, stop it." Tossing the curtain back, I walk to the end of the bed and flop back on the soft mattress.

I can't write. I don't want to go out of this room, and there's no TV in here. There's nothing to do but sleep. I close my eyes, but the sun's just barely crept below the horizon. There's no way I'll fall asleep. My mind goes into overdrive, sifting through thoughts about this damn book and Edwin, and then Jax and his smile and his dimples and muscles pop into my head, and there—my thoughts cease.

Something about Jax gets to me. I recall how I felt when, on the night I first met him, he told me I was beautiful. *Incredibly beautiful...* I don't take compliments well—always thinking it's a lie, something the person is doing just to dig at me—but for some reason, when he said it, I believed him. And that makes me uneasy. It makes me feel vulnerable because I don't let people get to me—not on *that* level. *It was because I was drunk. That has to be why it seemed natural.* A frustrated groan works its way up my throat.

Since the moment I laid eyes on him in that damn bar, I've had this crazy attraction to him. And it's not the superficial bullshit. It's not his rugged jawline or messy hair or those muscles evident even through his clothes. No, I think it's the fact that Jax is a walking, breathing oxymoron. He looks like the type of guy that would be an arrogant asshole, but he's awkward and uncomfortable and nervous. I'm not sure many people see that, but I do. And, above that, I think it might be his eyes that draw me in. I can see a profound level of depth in him—I can see twisted demons fighting behind that smile and those dimples. What fool can't appreciate dark things wrapped in pretty packages?

The longer I think about Jax, the more those innocent thoughts morph into the image of him with his hands in my hair, my back against a wall. I find myself wondering what his lips would feel like pressed against mine, his rough hands roaming my bare flesh. What he would look like between my thighs, his skin slicked with sweat, his chest rising in ragged swells. And before I realize it, I feel my hands playing out exactly where I want his hands on my body.

My fingers skim over my stomach. Goose bumps sweep over my skin before I shove down my jeans. I let one hand trail beneath my shirt to palm my breast while a finger from my other hand slowly slips beneath the waistband of my lace thong. I imagine Jax pinning me to the bed, his mouth working down my neck as he sweeps his fingers underneath the lacy material, feeling the reaction my body has to him. And that thought has me biting my lip with a soft moan. He'd slip one finger inside me then groan at how good I felt... my finger sinks inside me, then another, my legs falling shamelessly apart as I enjoy this little daydream.

He'd kiss me, and it would be brutal—his hand gripping my jaw before his fingers wound around my throat. He'd whisper what a dirty girl I am, what a filthy little slut he wants me to be for him, right before he'd end up with his head between my thighs. The thought of his mouth on me like that, my fingers tangled in his messy brown hair—that first warm lick would be enough to send me over the edge.

My heels dig into the mattress, my back bowing away from the bed as that blissful heat jolts through me. I fight the moan, tossing my head to the side and biting my lip as I give in to that feeling. And then, as soon as that heat dissipates, with my fingers still buried deep inside me, guilt slams over me.

I stare at the ceiling, my heart still slamming against my rib cage from the sudden release of endorphins as I pull up my jeans and fasten them. When I sit up, I sigh. This is what they mean by idle hands are the Devil's workshop, and I'm terrified the next time I see Jax, all I'm going to be able to think about is this—me playing with myself while thinking about him. It will be all over my face. I'll turn beet red the second I lay eyes on him.

My thoughts are cut off by the sound of the back door slamming. My pulse speeds up.

Footsteps come down the hall. There's a cough then a soft knock on the door. "Miranda?"

I swallow then unlock the door, praying my cheeks aren't still flushed when I pull it open. Clearing my throat, I force a smile. "Yep?"

"I know I'm a day early and that I promised not to bother you, but I was just struck with some *incredible* inspiration and was hoping you might be up for a little writing session." Edwin smiles, his dark eyes never leaving my own.

"Oh, um, yeah." I nod. I can feel sweat beading on my brow. "Sure."

"Well, I'm already in the office, and I've got a fresh pot of coffee going if you'd like to join me." He turns without waiting for a response and makes his way down the hall, humming "Singin' in the Rain."

Something about him is way off, almost like a weight has been lifted from his shoulders. Maybe that "incredible inspiration" came in the form of drugs.

He stops behind the desk and pulls my chair out for me. I eye him cautiously as I take a seat and turn on the desktop computer. And he's *still* humming. He takes his own seat, looks over at me, and smiles.

"I hope your spa day was as beneficial as my writing retreat was for me," he says, cracking his knuckles before powering up his computer.

"It was relaxing. Thank you, by the way. That was very

nice of you."

"Please, don't even mention it. I'm glad you enjoyed it." He turns, an eyebrow arched. "I noticed you all got back later in the afternoon. Enjoy the city a bit?"

Inhaling, I nod. "Yep. Janine took me to some diner. So... what are we writing?"

He looks at me as if he's trying to read me, studying me. He smiles once more, a slanted, unnatural smile, then turns his attention back to the screen. "Hmmm, well, we're right at the part where Deacon has captured his first victim. He's confused, angry, thirsty. Your girl..." He looks at me and smiles. "Your girl is obviously shit-scared." He laughs.

"Right." I glance at the screen, skimming over the last few paragraphs.

And he goes back to fucking humming. "So I think we just go through the natural progressions. He's got her in the house, bound to a bed. What's next? Does he torture her? Does he play with her? Or does he just get the deed over and done with?" He taps his chin, eyes to the ceiling. He finally puts a finger up and nods approvingly. "I think he fucks with her. It's his first kill. He won't be able to control himself."

Natural progressions? There's a natural progression to murder... and it evidently begins with torture. I clear my throat and look back at the computer screen, at the flashing cursor.

And then he begins to type.

I can barely believe my eyes. It's almost like a dream, like if I pinch myself, I'll come jolting from my sleep back to my hideously boring reality. But it's not a dream, and her trembling, naked body handcuffed to the bed frame is a nice little reminder of that. So is the smell of piss that's taken up the room since I started handling the hacksaw.

"What's wrong, sweetheart?" I lift the saw and shake it. "Just because I brought it doesn't mean I'll use it."

I smile and wink at her, then I look back at the table holding a duffel bag and all the tools I just pulled from it. I brought a lot with me. It's my first time, so I'm not really sure what I'll end up using. As I survey my inventory, a rush takes over me. I look back at her quivering on the dirty mattress, and I can't help but smile. Twenty-seven years have led to this day right here.

Edwin stops typing and glances at me with a curious look in his eye. "What would you say to him in this situation? Would you beg him?"

"I mean..." I drag in a breath. "I haven't ever really, um..." A slight smirk plays across his lips, and it leaves me unsettled. "I guess I would beg him. Try to make him see me as a person..."

"Haven't ever really what? Please, finish that sentence."

I swallow. Hard. "Uh, it's just that I've never really thought about what I would do, you know?"

He chuckles, shaking his head like a disappointed

father would. "Well, dear, this is fiction, and you are a fiction writer. If you ever hope to become something in this world, I hope you can find a way to put yourself in those positions. To dig and claw and fight for that inspiration. I've never been a detective either, but I've made millions writing them." He turns back to the screen, his head shaking again and his fingers hovering over the keyboard. "Don't worry about it. I've got this."

And he goes back to typing and humming. I watch him. Every so often a crooked smile forms on his lips, and I find myself wondering...

A relentless mix of both fear and exhilaration stirs in my head as I glide a finger over the jagged edges of the saw blade, my gaze fixed on her as I wait for a response.

"Please." She chokes on a sob. "Please, God. Please..." Her words are lost on a pitiful cry.

"God?" I smile, looking at the ceiling then back down at her. "Fuck God." I lean in, my mouth to her ear, and I can feel her breath against my neck. "God doesn't give a fuck about you... and neither do I." I pull back and laugh, tossing the hacksaw from one hand to the other.

She's crying so hard she chokes, gagging on her own goddamn tears. "I'll do whatever you want. I won't tell anyone. I promise. I swear. I swear..." Another long sob racks her body. "Just let me go. Please don't kill me. Please." Her eyes are riddled with tears, her plump lips quivering.

I pout, one of those exaggerated ones with the bottom lip sticking way out. "Oh dear, I wish I could help you. I really do. I've just waited too damn long for this."

She shakes her head, those beautiful tears cascading down her pale cheeks.

I slide the teeth of the hacksaw softly over her shackled leg, right at the ankle. Screaming, she fights to yank it away, the handcuffs jangling against the steel-framed bed.

"No point in screaming. No point at all. There's not a soul for miles."

I do it again, and she wails, coughing and choking. It's the look in her eyes—the wide-eyed horror swimming in her tear-filled eyes—that motivates me, propels me to feed the lust that has been burning inside me my entire miserable life.

The typing pauses for a second as he continues that constant humming, and he exhales, tapping his fingers over the desk. I glance at him out of the corner of my eye, and he's staring out that damn window. At that fucking shed. With a smile. And that lump forms in my throat.

When the hacksaw's teeth begin making a mess of her flesh, blood spurting from the gnarled skin, her eyes roll back in her head. She screams, a pointless cry that sends a wave of pleasure over me. I can feel my cock swell in my jeans. The thin skin at her ankle gives way to bone, which makes a much different sound when the hacksaw grinds through it. It's like a zipper being done and undone over and over and over again. Her foot is halfway off, veins shooting off like fire hoses, when I notice her face go pale. I set the hacksaw down next to her and walk gingerly to the duffel bag. I pull out a syringe, a vial of adrenaline, and four tourniquets.

Settling back down by her side, I first put on the tourniquet. Not above her ankle though. I set it all the way up near the hip so I can work my way up. Once the tourniquet is fastened, I fill a syringe with a bit of adrenaline, stick the vein in the crack of her bicep, and within seconds, she comes charging back to reality, her eyes bulging from her head and mouth gasping for air.

"Aw, there you are, sweetheart! Good to have you back. You can't go leaving me so soon. Our date has just started."

The humming stops, and Edwin pushes back from the desk with a pleased sigh. "Well, I'm tapped for now. Would you like to go get some food?"

I glance from him to the flashing cursor then back, wondering what the hell he even needed me here for. "Uh... yeah, yeah, sure thing. Let me just go grab my purse."

"No rush, I've got a few things to handle first anyways," he says with a grin before walking toward the front door, resuming that damn unnerving humming.

I scoot my chair away from the desk, the legs scraping over the hardwood floor, but my gaze strays to my computer screen. Chill bumps sweep over my skin as I read what Edwin so effortlessly wrote. It's so gruesome—and that humming and his wicked little smile while he was typing.

It's just a story.

Just words strung together to make thoughts, so I shouldn't feel this moral war waging inside me over what was just written. It doesn't make me sick or deranged that I like this, so it doesn't mean that Edwin is sick or deranged for writing it. It's just imagination... but what makes someone's imagination live in such dark places? What drives our stories to come from within the shadows? The more I watch him write these words, the more I'm a little scared that maybe something's not right with either one of us.

CHAPTER TWELVE
Jackson

"Only the Lonely"—Iggy Pop

There have been few moments in my life when a small light has shone inside me, like flashlights off in the dark and distant. The first time was at my first real job—bagging at the quick shop down the street from my house. I was fifteen. She was eighteen and a cashier. I never had her heart, but for one reckless summer, she had every bit of mine. Her complete rejection when I finally worked up the nerve to ask her out crushed my little, previously untarnished heart.

The second time was in college, after the war and all the shit that came with it. Heather Montgomery. I met her in my English lit class my first year at Chapel Hill. She was vibrant and fresh and... overwhelming. I spent two years with her, pretending like nothing was going on with me, like I wasn't quietly suffering, before it all came crashing down. When my little sister was murdered, she just couldn't handle all that came with her death, especially when the devastation from Joanna's murder came to full realization. I couldn't cope, and she couldn't help me cope.

I don't fucking blame her.

The third time I felt that little flicker of light was two days ago when I had coffee with Miranda. She left me craving more conversation, more eyes lingering where they shouldn't. It's not like I can help myself. She's everything a warm-blooded male could want, all wrapped up in an awkward, irresistible package.

I'm a detective, and even I can't read this woman, and I think that's what intrigues me the most. She holds back so much but then gives away just enough. Just enough to make me want more. To keep her in my thoughts.

There are times in this life when the puzzle pieces start to fit. The universe lines up just enough. Times when the sun finally rises. It's hope. It's destiny. And in all my rotten years, and the handful of good ones, I haven't felt that often, but she stirs it in me. All my pain and confusion and hope—it's her burden too. My desperation, my acceptance, my drive? I see it in her. I see it in her eyes. I read it in her shoulders, her timidity, her doubt. And that makes the desire burn in me like a fuse inching toward detonation.

As my finger hovers over the Call button, Miranda's name on the iPhone screen, I can't help but think about just how much I'll fuck this up. If not now... certainly later.

I inevitably press my shaky finger against the button, but I get voicemail right away. I freeze, completely clueless as to how I should proceed. Actually leaving a message would be a good start, but as her sweet, delicate voice comes through the line in her message, words become useless to me. I'm a victim of my own complete inadequacy. The beep comes across the line, and I babble what is likely incoherent shit and hang up as quickly as I can.

Setting my phone back on the nightstand, I exchange it for the latest EA novel, *Cry of the Afflicted*. It got blasted in the reviews, but I absolutely love it. This is my third time through, and I'm still finding new shit in it. Halfway in and I'm devouring it as if it's the first time all over again. Most of the reviewers hated the book because it was too brutal... and of course because the antagonist won in the end. If it's not happily ever after these days, people lose their shit. I enjoyed the fact that he changed it up. Why should the detective win every time anyways?

I open the book and set the bookmark on the bed, losing myself in the words and doing my best to remove Miranda from my thoughts.

There's a hideous gurgle that sounds only when a throat has been slit. It's the only thing really that can make me cringe. I don't often operate this way, but the bitch just wouldn't shut up. I've had criers in my years of killing—screamers too—but this woman, she was something else. Like a fucking banshee, gnashing and clawing as I attempted to put the ball gag on her. I hadn't tied the rope tight enough, that's for sure, but I hadn't planned on the amount of drugs this bitch must've taken beforehand. And the ridiculous strength it gave her.

As she bleeds out in the tub, grasping at her throat with both hands, I can't help but feel sad I couldn't have had more fun with her before it came to this. A surge of anger rushes over me. How could she fuck this up for me with her relentless shrieking? How could she take away my pleasure in causing pain? Impulsively, and without another thought, I lift the hunting knife and thrust it down into her left eye socket. Her remaining eye bulges out as her tied hands come down on her face, wildly batting at nothing in particular. She arches her back, trying her best to pull her head away, but she can't. She is mine for the taking. And I will see to it that she suffers as much as possible before the blood loss inevitably takes her.

I pull the hunting knife out, and the slurping sound it creates oddly reminds me of those bright summer days of my youth when Dad would cut up watermelon for the family. With another quick thrust, I take out her right eye. Her arms freefall to the porcelain tub with a thud, *the blood from her neck now running instead of gushing, and I take a few steps back, straightening myself and dropping my head to the side. I set the blade of the knife lightly to my temple, and for a quiet, serene moment, I admire my handiwork in all its filthy, fucked-up glory.*

CHAPTER THIRTEEN
Miranda

"I Really Want You to Hate Me"—Meg Myers

I stand beneath the green-and-white awning, my eyes lifting to the sign: *Ristorante Maestrale.*

I smooth my skirt as I make my way up the stairs, weaving through the crowd gathered around the open door. The hostess standing just inside the entrance smiles and grabs a menu, starting to turn from the podium.

"Uh, there will be two," I say with a scowl.

"Oh..." She reaches behind her and grabs another menu. "Sorry."

I follow her through the crowded dining room to a booth at the very back of the restaurant.

"There you go. Right by the window," she says, the clinking of dishes and the lull of conversation nearly drowning out her mousy voice. I take a seat, and she places the menu in front of me before setting the other on the table. "Is there a name I should be waiting for to show them where you've been sat?" A slight smirk forms on her lips.

"Uh, a guy... a man. About six foot tall. Brown hair." I shrug. I should just give her his name, but for some reason, I just don't want to. Maybe it's embarrassment. Or worry. I don't want her to think I'm some slut of his. "I'm sure he'll find me."

She arches a brow before turning on her heel and walking off.

Just as I open the menu, my phone dings with a voicemail. The first thought that runs through my mind is that it's most likely my pathetic mother calling to beg me for more money. Rolling my eyes, I press Play, wondering whether she'll be strung out on meth or just drunk this time.

"Uh... hey, Miranda. It's... uh... Jax. Just wanted to see what you were doing. Thinking maybe dinner was in order. Call me back when you're... um... when you're not busy."

I don't even realize I'm smiling until I catch my reflection in the window. I exit out of my voicemail and set my phone on the table, staring at it. My gaze drifts out the window in search of Edwin then back to the phone. I don't do this entire people thing—guy thing—whatever this is, so I'm not really sure whether calling him back this soon will make me look desperate or not. And besides, what am I going to say? *Come hang out with me and the raging dickhead?* Nope, I'll just stumble over my words. I shake my head and drop my phone inside my purse. And *this* is why I want to write. You don't have to know how to deal with people. Only imaginary people.

A young, acne-riddled waiter stops at the end of the table, sucking me out of my thoughts. "Would you like something to drink, ma'am?"

"Water." I look at the empty seat across from me. "I guess two waters."

"Any wine this evening?"

I shake my head, and he turns to walk away, but I stop him. "You know what? Yeah, give me a glass of chardonnay, please."

"House?"

"That's fine."

I bury my face in my palms as he walks off. This entire ordeal with Edwin is stressing me out, and the fact that Jax has, for whatever fucking reason, taken up residence in my head... so what will a glass of wine hurt?

A few moments later, the waiter returns with a large glass of wine, which I down in a matter of minutes. Every few minutes the waiter passes by, glancing at the empty seat. He brings me a second glass of wine—and a third—and still I sit alone, my fingers drumming over the white tablecloth.

The waiter stops at the table again, this time balancing a tray of dirty dishes on his arm. "You sure you don't want to order an appetizer while you wait? Some calamari, possibly?"

"Uh, yeah. I'm sure." I glance at the empty seat,

STEVIE J. COLE & BT URRUELA

embarrassment nearly drowning me. *Where the hell is he?*

I smile as the waiter walks off, and for some reason, the room starts to feel as though it's closing in on me. The conversation grows louder. The rattle of dishes. The annoying laugh of that lady across the room. The child whining. Whining. Whining. Sweat begins to prick over my forehead, and my head is swimming from the wine. I just need to step outside for a moment. Get a breath of fresh air. Not have that damn waiter staring at me because I'm here alone and waiting like a woman who's been stood up. I don't want him to think I'm *that* girl, so I push away from the table, grabbing my phone and purse, and briskly make my way to the front and out the door.

The cold air wraps around me, loosening the tension that has been building in my muscles like a small tremor. I take a deep breath. I glance around the crowded parking lot, telling myself Edwin is roaming around looking for a parking spot. Maybe he's been stopped by fans.

Telling myself I'm not crazy for continuing to work with him. That it will all work out in the end.

My heels tap over the pavement as I make my way back to the entrance of the restaurant. My cheeks sting from the warmth from inside. I skirt around the hostess stand, weave between the family of four blocking the opening to the dining area, and go straight to my table.

There's a fresh glass of water. I fall down into the chair and grab my phone before I set my purse in the empty seat beside me.

Jax. Jax and his dimples. He wants to see me. I want to see him. No, if I'm honest, I want to do more than see him, and for that, I am ashamed. I want him naked on top of me, his hands wrapped tightly around my throat as he fucks me. I feel a slight pressure build between my thighs at the thought of it, and almost as suddenly as that desire has begun to torch through me like a rogue fire amongst parched woods, guilt douses me. Something about him makes me feel slightly mad. Unhinged in the most delightful of ways. He makes me feel as if I could possibly be something I'm not. As if I could be *that* girl. *That* girl authors write about. *That* girl readers dream they were. *That* girl who ends up with *that* guy...

My leg is shaking, and I've nearly chewed through my bottom lip. I pull up his contact, staring at his name. His name: Jax Peralta. Something about that sounds so right. Miranda and Jax. I feel like a teenager again with a ridiculous crush. My finger hovers over the Call button. Anticipation builds. My heart pounds in my chest; my mouth feels dry.

"More wine?"

I barely hear the waiter I'm so focused on my phone, but I nod all the same, and he trots off.

No, texting is easier because then I don't have to talk to him and worry about what a bumbling idiot I sound like. I can just type out words, read them, realize how ridiculous they sound, and delete the entire message. Gone—like I never even thought those things.

I quickly type: *Hey. Saw that you called. What's up?*

Shaking my head, I bury my face in my palms, peeking through my fingers with one eye as I go to delete that stupid message, and somehow, my fumbling fingers hit the Call button.

I panic and grab the phone. Just as I go to hang up, I hear the muffled sound of his deep voice come over the line, and I cringe, biting my lip as I lift the phone to my ear.

"Well, how about that. A call back from Miranda. How you been?" Jax says.

My heart goes into an immediate sprint, heat creeping over every last inch of my skin. "Good," I blurt. I take a breath, praying for my voice not to shake. "Got your message, and uh, I was just, you know, calling you back."

The waiter places the glass of wine on the table. I grab it and take a large gulp just as an elderly couple shuffles past the table, the woman talking so loudly I can't help but be distracted from the call.

"Glad you did. It's good to hear from you." He hesitates. "Given any thought to dinner?"

"Well, actually. I'm *at* dinner..."

"Wait, wait, wait... tell me you called me while you're out to dinner with EA Mercer. Even if you gotta lie, give me that win."

A small smile tears at my lips. "Yeah, I'm with the

raging dick."

He laughs, and it carries loudly over the line. "Raging dick or not, I love his words. Reading his latest right now actually and wondering when I'm going to be able to get his next one. I heard he got himself a killer co-author. Wink. Wink."

I feel my cheeks heat, and I'm giggling like a thirteen-year-old girl. "Well, I'll see what I can—" I catch Edwin in my peripheral just before he plops down in the booth across from me.

He flashes me a smile as he smooths out his shirt, then he eyes the phone in my hand.

"Oh, hey, you know what, let me call you later. Edwin just sat down."

A snicker comes across the line, and it's now Jax who sounds like the prepubescent teen. "Did you really just call him Edwin? Un-*fucking*-real." He laughs. "Okay, okay, call me later."

I hang up and slide the phone back inside my purse, my face still on fire.

Edwin's cheeks are flushed, his skin damp. "Sorry for the delay, I couldn't find parking to save my life."

"Yeah, it's crowded in here." I narrow my gaze on him as I pick up the menu. "You okay?"

Nodding, he lets out a heavy sigh. "You'd think the nicest restaurant in this city would have some fucking valet. And a better-looking hostess." He laughs and motions back toward the entrance. "You see that fucking bitch? Obnoxious little one, she is."

"Uh..." I grimace. He's such an asshole and so disgustingly inappropriate. It almost makes me wonder how in the hell he's become so successful. "So what's good anyway?"

"What's good?" He recoils, curling his lip in disgust. "What are you, fifteen? Come now." He shakes his head as his eyes drop to the menu. He abruptly lets the menu fall to the table and grabs the top of my hand, giving it a squeeze. He has a saccharine sweet smile. "What am I going to do with you?"

My jaw clenches, and I clear my throat as I pull my hand away from his grip. "I meant, what do you suggest, Edwin?"

He doesn't respond right away. His eyes are locked on his hand, now alone on the white tablecloth. "What do you think of our book?" His eyes trail up my body until they meet mine. "I mean really."

"I think it's good."

"Good? *Just* good?" he asks, no emotion in his voice.

"I mean"—I feel sweat building beneath my hair—"it's—"

"Because I think it's great." He smiles, pulling his hand back finally, clasping it with his other hand. "I think it's exceptional."

That's not what I'd expected. I'm almost taken aback

by his compliment. "I really like it. I think the characters work well together. Our writing is complementary."

"I think you and I make a great team," he says. It's almost as though he didn't even hear what I said. "If this book does as well as I think it will, there's potential for many more after it. I've shared what we've written already with my publishers. Janine's read it too. They're all smitten with Ms. Miranda Cross." The crooked smile inching its way across his lips makes a knot form in the pit of my stomach. "As smitten as I've found myself." His smile deepens.

I swallow as an uneasy laugh makes its way up my throat.

He unlocks his fingers and picks up his menu once again. He opens it and hums as he scans the words. "I like the filet a lot, but really, you can't go wrong with any of the meat on their menu. They have an in-house butcher." A wry smile curves across his lips. "Cut fresh daily." Then he winks at me, his eyes locking with mine.

And it's in this moment I wish I were more practiced with social skills, more apt at figuring people out. Because in that stare, while he's attempting to make it warm, is something so cold and uncalculated. Or maybe, maybe that's a look of diverging motivations between he and me. I swallow, my eyes darting from his and down to the menu, which is now subtly shaking in my nervous hands. For some reason, I feel like small, helpless prey, and he's the hunter waiting in the bushes for the moment I step onto the snare he's so carefully laid out.

But, really, that's ridiculous...

"Ma'am?" The waiter stops at the table, his eyes darting nervously to Edwin's seat. "Would you like to go ahead and order?"

"Yes, yes, we would," I say.

He smiles nervously, jots down the order, and walks away. And I'm left here with Edwin. To awkward conversation and my own overactive imagination wondering exactly *what* he wants from me.

CHAPTER FOURTEEN
Edwin

"Doomed"—Bring Me the Horizon

There are skeletons in every closet. In some, they're stacked ceiling-high. In this world, you're either predator or prey, and it's all predetermined. As predetermined as retardation or cancer. Those of us ingrained with the will to live, to survive, to thrive, and to kill if we must, we see the world for what it is. We understand the wicked within us all. We harness it.

The wicked side of me will always be the most powerful, and I think that's where I differ from most other alphas. I don't have a stopping point. I have no moral compass. I am not guided by unseen bullshit. I am the God of my own world, waiting for the outer world to crumble around me so I may laugh upon its ruins.

What if I told you we live, we die, and then nothing else? What if I told you I saw it coming long ago in a dream? I saw myself morphing, evolving into a beast, feeding off the fire and brimstone... the end of days... the forgotten souls. With each step, the earth shook in devastating fashion. I breathed fire onto the huddled remaining few. I watched their skin peel from their bones. And in the destruction, I became full.

Now, I find myself in this peculiar position, this position of fucking weakness, and one I have never found myself in before—wanting another human being for more than just blood or a fuck. As of late, my mind wanders to Miranda so often, and though I could fuck her to within an inch of her life, that's not what drives me insane. It's the desire to be near her, to love her, to make her mine. I knew it from the moment I saw her name... and the moment I read her words. She was meant to be with me, and I with her.

I thought about that phone call the whole dinner. The deep male voice over the line. The red in her face as she spoke to him. I tried my best to hold in my anger, to act normal, but it's fucking boiling inside me.

My hands grip the steering wheel so tightly my knuckles turn ghost white. Silence fills the car as it has since we left the restaurant, and if it continues, I just might run this fucking car into oncoming traffic.

"So who was that on the phone?" I ask—I blurt it, really.

"When?"

When? Bitch, don't act like you don't know what I'm talking about. "At dinner."

"Oh, a friend..." Her eyes narrow, the light from street lamps flicking over her pale skin as we barrel down the highway. "I guess maybe an acquaintance. I don't know." She glances out of the window. "He's a really big fan of yours."

My mind starts to sketch out what *he* might look like, what their connection is, what he could give her that I can't. "Oh yeah? Big fan, you say? I'll have to sign a book for him," I say, fighting back the urge to find out more about this *friend*.

"That would be really nice of you." She glances at me and smiles.

"I've always held the belief that men and women can't really be friends. One party always wants to fuck the other," I say, glancing at her with an eyebrow raised and a coy smile. "But who the hell am I to say? I don't have any friends."

"Well"—she crosses her arms—"I disagree. Not everything's about fucking, you know?"

I laugh, finding her naivety amusing. "Oh, dear, don't you know? The world revolves around money and fucking."

She glares at me, arms still crossed. "For certain people..." A smirk dances over her red lips. "I'm sure it does."

"I suppose love *is* in the mix somehow." I look at her out of the corner of my eye. "Tell me, Miranda, have you ever been in love?"

She laughs, shaking her head, her hair falling softly over her shoulders as my fingers beg to get tangled in it. "Love is a crock of shit."

A sudden burst of laughter erupts from my mouth. I slap the steering wheel hard a few times. "I feel I may have underestimated you. Here I was thinking you were the glass-half-full type."

"Yeah, well, I can assure you I'm not."

"I do believe in love. As black as my little heart may be, I do believe in this world, there is someone for every asshole." I pull the car off the county round and onto the long, pitch-black driveway leading to my cabin. "It's just a matter of stumbling into them. And not *ever* letting them slip away."

"Well, if that's the case, I've yet to stumble across *my* asshole, I guess." She shakes her head.

I loop the car around the front of the cabin and park just to the side of it. Opening my door, I nearly trip over myself trying to get over to Miranda's side fast enough to open the door for her. She's got it halfway open by the time I get to the passenger's side, but I hold it for her regardless. She'll like that.

She looks up at me. "Oh, thanks..."

She steps out and slips past me. I trail her to the front door, my eyes tracing the curve of her ass, lost in the thought of what kind of underwear she's wearing. And the thought of them balled up and stuffed into her mouth.

141

No. I don't want to hurt her. How could I? *I love her.*

I unlock the front door and open it, letting her go in first before I follow. The cabin is completely still and dark. *Perfect.*

She flips the switch on the wall, and the front room lights up. Her eyes drift from my face, down my body. She wants me, and she's making it evident. I smile until her gaze stops on my legs, her eyes widening and her brow scrunching.

"Edwin..." she says softly.

I look down to the exact place her gaze has landed. *Blood.* In spots near my knee.

"Is that..." Her eyes narrow. "Is that..." Her perfect little brows pinch together, shooting a jolt of want through me. "Is that blood?"

I laugh, shaking my head and drawing my focus back to her. "How funny is that? Cut myself the other day chopping wood." I hold up my thumb and flash an inch-long gash down the side. It's a few days healed, and it was from an ax all right, but I wasn't chopping wood. "It busted back open earlier today. Must not have noticed." I shrug and flash her a toothy smile. "Though I guess you didn't notice either, did you?"

Stepping back, she shakes her head. "No, I didn't." A smile flinches over her lips, followed by a short, uncertain laugh. "Well, good night." She turns on her heel and heads toward the hallway.

"Good night, Miranda," I call as she disappears into the darkness.

She doesn't see it, but I'm smiling. I'm smiling because there's a yearning inside me, alive and feeding off of her, growing in intensity with each passing day. I want her. I need her. And with every drop of willpower I can muster, I fight the urge to follow her into her room, take what I've wanted all this time, and give her what she wants in return. I know she yearns for me too. How could she not? It's only a matter of time before I make her mine.

It's only a matter of time before we kill as one.

CHAPTER FIFTEEN
Jackson

"Cry Little Sister"—Gerard McMann

"How fresh?" I ask Tommy as we cross the busy street, evening rush hour well under way. I cradle a full coffee—probably my twentieth of the day—in both hands as Tommy manhandles two donuts. I stopped counting those around lunchtime.

"Examiners think within the last twenty-four. They figured we'd want to get a look at it before they carted her off." He chuckles, his mouth full of pastry. "It's a mess, partner."

"So I've been told. You said an abandoned house off Twelfth, right?" I ask just as we meet the intersection of Twelfth and Stark.

"Yeah." He points at a decrepit house a few hundred feet away blocked off by police tape with a clutter of personnel spread out around the area. Curious neighbors have taken to their porches. Tommy chuckles again, swallowing the last of his donut. "Fuckin' stray dog pulled the bitch's foot out of the house and into the street. That's how they fuckin' found her."

"You shitting me?"

"Do I ever?"

I just roll my eyes. I never know what to believe when it's coming out of Tommy's mouth.

"She's in about ten different pieces, partner. Scout's honor." He does a jacked-up Boy Scout salute then holds up the police tape for me to go underneath.

I nod in appreciation then pass a few more nods to some of the personnel I'm fond of, mingling in the front yard.

"Hacked up at every joint," he continues, "and at the neck. I mean, we're talking Mr. Potato Head type shit in there."

"Keep your voice down, you jackass." I roll my eyes as I pass through the doorway, the door itself hanging by one hinge. "It's been way too long of a day for that shit."

"Just speaking the truth, man. You'll see. She's like a human jigsaw puzzle." He laughs and slaps the back of his hand against my arm. "Like human Tetris." He laughs.

"Fuck off, man," I say, pulling away from him just as we come up on the body.

He wasn't lying. Not one fucking bit. There are two loaded up trash bags, each with shredded holes torn in the side. A trail of blood is smeared from the bags and tracked out into the hallway. Congealed fat, yellow and pungent, protrudes from the openings, along with bits of mangled, bloody flesh. I make out a hand too, purplish-blue fingers poking out from beneath the sludgy mess.

I step back, taking a much needed breath of fresh air from the other room, then go back in. Tommy stands in the corner of the room with two medical examiners, a stupid toothy smile on his face. I approach one of the bags and crouch, making sure to breathe only through my mouth, though I worry about what particles I'm picking up that way too. The thought turns my stomach. I pull a pen from my pocket and use the end of it to tug the bag open wider.

I wish I hadn't. The mostly untarnished face of a young brunette stares back at me. Her dead eyes bulge a bit from her head, skin and veins mushrooming from her severed neck, but otherwise, she looks like she probably had before all this happened to her... with a little rigor mortis added in the mix.

And she looks like my sister.

From the dark curls matted to her head with blood, to the blue-gray tint of her eyes, she's a spitting image of Joanna. And it reminds me of that day two years ago, when I found my sister in three pieces in a house not far from here. She had the same knifed-out Xs on her breasts that I'm sure to find on this young lady, just as I've found on many of the other victims along the way.

I close my eyes, my pulse quickening. My stomach lurches. My thoughts are owned by my sister, back when she was still that smiling, carefree girl, back before the drugs dried up all the life in her. When this monster got to her, she was just a shell of who she once was, but it hurt all the same.

If my parents were still alive, I would've surely gotten the blame somehow. *You should've been there! Aren't you a cop?*

It doesn't matter. I put the blame on myself anyway. I heap it onto my shoulders right along with the PTSD and alcoholism, along with the failed relationships and the thousands of little lies I've told myself over the years—and the ones I still do.

I stand abruptly, so quick a rush of blood leaves my brain and makes me stumble.

"Partner, you okay?" Tommy asks, putting a hand on my elbow to stabilize me.

"Y-yeah, I-I'm good." I look at him through clouded vision, blinking in an attempt to clear it. "You mind wrapping this up, Tommy? I've seen enough for today."

He gives me two good pats on the back as he leads me out of the room. "I got you, buddy. You definitely ain't looking so good."

"I'm all right. Just haven't eaten today yet." We reach the door, and I turn to face him. "I'm gonna go grab a bite and take some time to myself. You sure you're all right wrapping this up?"

"Too easy, partner. Too easy. Take your time. I'll start

the paperwork on this shit." He jabs a thumb back toward the garbage bags now being carefully emptied by the examiners, their contents sorted out on a tarp.

"Thanks." I turn and head out the door, pulling a pack of cigarettes from my pocket, a pack I've held on to for when I catch my sister's killer, but right about now, I just don't fucking care. I need it.

I take off the cellophane wrapping, shake out a cigarette, and light it, taking the smoke deep into my lungs as a fall breeze whips past me. I let the smoke dance out of my lungs with a pleasing sigh. Six months I've held on to this pack. Six months since I had my last cigarette. The cigarette's staleness does nothing to override the complete satisfaction I feel as a buzz carries through my body.

———

It's funny how the first day I smoke a cigarette in six months is the same day I attend church for the first time in ten years. God and I, we have a unique relationship. A little bit of love and a whole lot of hate... on my side only, of course. It's not that I blame him for my woes, because I don't. I just wonder sometimes why I couldn't have had it just a little bit different. Just a little bit better.

I couldn't help but to walk in as I was passing by, the preacher's voice carrying from the church. Calling to me. Before I knew what I was doing, my ass was in this pew, my cold heart despising every second of it.

I've always been a good man. I've always put others

first. Yet since the day I was fucking born, I've been shit on. There comes a time when you stop blaming yourself, and guess what? The blame's gotta go somewhere. I'm a God-fearing man, I always will be, so any blasphemous outbursts could be counted on one hand. But in my head, I'm cursing him all day long. Not so much for myself, but mostly for my sister, who truly was a happy girl.

She loved life, and there were a lot of times I was envious of her complete lack of self-pity.

Then the drugs found her, then prostitution, and then she was gone. I was left to sweep up the scraps of my life, to view the vast wasteland around me where my family should've been.

My hands rest on top of the pew in front of me, and I settle my head onto my arms. I feel as if an invisible hand is gripping my heart and pulling it slowly up through my throat. I can feel the force of my faith tearing a hole through me, along with all my doubts, insecurities, and fear.

"If you'll read along with me in Corinthians 1:27 and 28," the preacher says in his best infomercial delivery. "'God has chosen the world's insignificant and despised things—the things viewed as nothing—so He might bring to nothing the things that are viewed as something.'" He sets his Bible on the podium and scans the pews before him. "God does not choose the wise. He chooses the wicked and weary. He chooses those who are looked down upon, turned away, disregarded."

I slide down the pew and quietly stand. Having had more than enough, I shuffle down the aisle as the preacher continues.

"And He chooses them to do His work. To spread His message and His love. Through him, all things are possible."

I give one last passing glance to the crucified Jesus hanging above the door before I exit the church, heading first to A-1 liquor, then I go back to the department, back to the bloodshed, back to the looked down upon, the turned away... the disregarded who make up my homicide reports.

CHAPTER SIXTEEN
Miranda

"Possum Kingdom"—The Toadies

Ever since dinner the other night, Edwin has been—well, not very Edwin.

This morning, he's been overly nice: pulling out my chair every time I sit to write, making me coffee, and he hasn't mentioned the word "fate" a hundred times. To be honest, had I not spent time with him prior to today, I would probably think he's a charmer, but this is such a drastic change it's nothing less than unnerving.

Constantly staring at me, he's always trying to make eye contact, and I can't stomach it because those eyes of his, they're—I wouldn't call them demonic. No, they're dead. Empty. Absolute voids of nothingness. And the way he watches me with that slight smirk... it's as though he's sizing me up, trying to determine how he can go about using me only to destroy me. Maybe I'm paranoid or losing touch with reality. I am wired to jump to the most morbid of conclusions. I mean, James in the bookstore—I was convinced he wanted to kill me at one point.

I pace the length of my bedroom, trying to sort this out because I can't concentrate enough to write a single sentence with this pile of shit buzzing around in my head. Just because the man is being nice—and comes across creepy as hell while doing so—it doesn't mean anything. It doesn't.

I've spent the better half of the afternoon avoiding him, trying to convince myself that I've just let my overactive imagination run wild with me. Telling myself I only feel so uneasy being alone in this cabin with him because I don't allow myself to ever trust anyone—that I'm the one with a problem, not him. But this knot in my stomach, the way my hair stands on end when he subtly brushes his hand along the small of my back in passing, I don't know how much longer I can ignore that. Gut instinct is there for a reason—a deep, ingrained survival instinct that is probably not wise to ignore for as long as I have. *I just need to get out of this damn cabin. Clear my head. Escape... stop it, Miranda!*

Taking a deep breath, I open the door to my room and head down the hallway toward the kitchen. The stereo's blaring in the living room. Edwin's in the kitchen singing along to The Toadie's "Possum Kingdom," and—I swear—he gets louder every time the word "die" comes around in the chorus.

I turn the corner, only one foot across the threshold of

the kitchen, and I find Edwin leaning over the counter. His white apron is splattered with blood, a huge, wet stain to the right of the smiling cartoon lobster printed over the middle. A carving knife is clutched in his right hand. Shocked, I grab the wall to steady myself, a small gasp leaving my lips.

He's still bent over the counter when he slowly turns his head to look at me. A sly grin inches across his mouth as he straightens up a touch, takes the knife, and places it over a chunk of blood-soaked meat. "You sure do startle easily." He glances back at the mess on the counter. "It's just a fresh kill." There's a long pause. The grin on his face deepens—I think, or maybe I imagine it. "Venison has the highest level of iron out of all meats, you know?"

My heart sits in my throat. With each hard pound, my vision pulses. My mouth has gone dry, and I swallow before I clear my throat. "Is that so?"

He arches his brow and nods as he works at cutting a filet, which he drops on the counter. The wet, slapping sound makes my stomach lurch.

"Did you need something?" he asks.

"Uh..." Another quick swallow. "No, I just, um..." My gaze darts to the phone on the wall beside him. "I was just gonna call Janine."

He stops cutting the meat and glances back at me, his empty eyes boring into me.

"Just, uh..." I stall. My breathing grows ragged.

Uneven. *Think, Miranda. Fucking think.* "I just need some stuff from the market. I'm out of, um... out of toiletries and stuff like that. Want me to pick you up anything?"

One side of his mouth kicks up. "No, dear." His eyes slowly drag down my body, and chill bumps sweep across my skin. "Don't need anything from the market." And he goes back to hacking away at the meat, singing along to the song.

Nodding, I scoot behind him, my nerves on edge. I take the receiver from the wall and quickly jab Janine's number into the keypad. Adrenaline is pumping through my body, and my senses are heightened. I guess that's why I can literally hear the shredding sound of that knife tearing through the meat. For a fleeting moment, while the phone is ringing, my mind gets away from me. All I can see is Edwin in his damn apron, going at me with that knife as his dead eyes stare into mine. I imagine he'd be shouting for me to look at him. Angry. Filled with rage—

"Hello?" Janine's voice is a welcome distraction from my thoughts.

"Hey, Janine. Would you be able to take me into town for a few? I, uh, I need some stuff from the market and maybe some Starbucks or dinner or something." That feeling that someone is staring at you washes over me, and I cut my eyes to the side to find Edwin watching me, twirling that damn carving knife.

"Absolutely, honey. Give me half an hour to get

washed up, and I'll head that way."

"Okay. Thanks."

I hang up the phone and turn around just as Edwin tosses his head back and holds up a piece of raw meat, dangling it between his thick fingers. He opens his mouth. The chunk of meat falls inside, and a satisfied groan rumbles from his throat. Dropping his chin, his eyes lock with mine as he chews then makes an exaggerated swallow. One brow arches as he sticks his fingers in his mouth—one by one—to lick the blood from them.

"Jesus... Jesus..." he sings along with the song, and the blood drains from my head down to my toes, that weightless feeling nearly knocking me to the floor.

"So I'll be back later. We may have dinner in town, and I'll just, uh..." I skirt around him, and he turns, following my every move like a fucking predator stalking prey. "I just need to decompress. Can we pick up on writing tomorrow? I mean, if that's okay with you?"

I'm to the doorway by the time he answers. "Anything you want, my dear Miranda, is more than fine with me."

"Thanks," I blurt as I make my way through the living room and down the hall.

I gently close the door to my room, locking it before I take a deep breath. Anything can seem creepy as fuck if you make it. Anything can seem like a scene out of a book if you want it to. But that—*that* little encounter—was too much like the stories I've fallen in love with.

I grab my purse from the dresser, stopping to stare at my reflection. All the color has washed from my face. My eyes are wide with fear, my chest rising in uneven swells. *It's only fiction. Just words. Only words...*

———

I stare at the bottles of shampoo in a daze, replaying the sight of Edwin and that piece of raw meat in my head. A woman in an oversized T-shirt reaches in front of me for some shampoo, and that snaps me back to reality for the moment.

"Honey, it's not that hard of a decision." Janine grabs a pink bottle, pops the top, and inhales, her eyes fluttering back in her head. "I go by smell and smell alone. With my shampoo *and* my men." She laughs and places the shampoo back on the shelf then grabs another bottle. "Oh, or you can go by the name. 'Big Sexy Hair.'" She smiles. "Anything with sex in the name sells me." She tosses the bottle into the shopping cart. "There you go. All done. We can leave now."

Using her hip, Janine nudges her way between the cart and me and starts down the aisle toward the checkout. I grab the buggy, pushing it beside her, watching men eye us as we pass by. Janine pulls off the professional workingwoman thing when she wants to, but she does so with a touch of sexuality. Her blouse is always undone one button too low. Her pencil skirts are tight, clinging to curves most women would die for. And she has that fuck-me glance down.

We stop at checkout line nine. Janine snaps her fingers. The bag boy runs around the counter, immediately unloading the items from the buggy onto the conveyor belt, a huge smile plastered over his face as he stares at me. Why me instead of Janine, I have no idea...

"So you just wanted out of that cabin, didn't you, honey?" A knowing smile crosses her face, and she shrugs. "Has he been an asshole again?"

"Uh, no. Actually, he's been nice, like overly nice."

Her brows knit together. "Nice? EA... *nice*?"

I nod, my gaze drifting off to the rack of tabloids. There's a moment of silence, with the exception of the constant beep from the cashier scanning the groceries.

"Huh," Janine says, placing her hand on her hip and turning around to face me. I glance at her, and she's giving me a once-over, a slight grin creeping over her red lips. "Well, EA, maybe you aren't asexual after all." She chuckles before spinning back around.

I push the cart to the end of the line. "What?" I take my wallet from my purse and hand the cashier my debit card.

"I thought he was one of those guys who just didn't have sex or, you know, maybe just was happy using his hand, a bottle of Vaseline Intensive Care, and a sock."

"Oh, God, Janine..."

The cashier's eyes widen. She glances between Janine

and me as she hands me the receipt.

"Wonder what kind of porn that one's into."

"I don't want to know. I don't need to know." I shake my head.

The bag boy takes charge of the shopping cart. Janine and I follow him out of the automatic doors to the parking lot. The sun is just beginning to lower in the gray autumn sky, and the chill in the air makes my skin prickle.

"Look at you." Janine elbows me in the side just before we stop behind the trunk of her car. "Catching the eye of Mr. Happy himself." She giggles so hard she snorts. "I mean, he may be an asshole, but he *is* a good-looking man. Can't deny that. And the quiet ones are always the ones that'll pull your hair and give you a good choking."

"There's no way in hell—"

"Oh, come on."

"Shit, Janine. Have you slept him or something?"

"I mean, I won't say it didn't cross my mind a time or two after a bottle of vodka." A snarl slowly forms over her lips. "Debated it heavily one time. I blame tequila for that one, but I don't shit where I eat, you know? That causes way too much of a mess." She shrugs. "You? You write this book with him, and you don't have to ever see him again. You could fuck him the last night you're there. Tell me if it's any good then go on your merry way knowing you got piped down by a *New York Times* best seller. I mean, it's just sex, you know? And if it's good sex..."

"Yeah, I'll pass," I mumble, staring at her. I'm amazed at how blunt she is, but I'm more confused by the fact that she's trying to talk me into sleeping with the creeper.

The bag boy finishes unloading the groceries then slams the trunk. "You okay, ma'am? Need any more help?"

I shake my head, hand him a ten, and he leaves with a smile.

"I don't feel like driving. I've got a headache from hell that only alcohol can cure." Janine moans and tosses me her keys. "Do you mind?"

Shaking my head, I climb into the car and crank the engine.

Janine slams the passenger side door and gently squeezes my thigh, a deadpan look on her face. "Tell me, are *you* asexual, honey?"

"What?"

"I mean, you've been up here for a few weeks. EA's got a hard-on for you, and you aren't interested. Then that sex-on-legs in the bar—Pax, Jax, whatever the hell his name was—was it Jax?"

I nod.

"Well," she says with a snort, "you couldn't have seemed more disinterested."

I shake my head. "What? I don't know how I could've been more obvious." I think back to the blatant way I was staring at him, and my cheeks grow warm with embarrassment.

"Really? Oh, honey." She pats my face. "Going all googly-eyed at a man? Is that the best you got?" She sighs as I put the car in reverse. "You authors are such a weird breed. You'd think with overactive imaginations like you people have to have that you'd be able to woo the robe off a Tibetan monk." She sighs. "Jesus, I could only imagine how awkward an actual relationship between two socially challenged authors like you and EA would be." She shudders a little.

"You know, I feel like I should be offended by that."

"Probably," she laughs. "You said EA had been nice. Why don't you tell me what EA has done that qualifies as 'nice,' because I am really intrigued to see what *his* wooing abilities are like."

"He's not trying to woo me." I swallow.

"Uh-huh, because men aren't always thinking about sex? Let's see... EA... I'd imagine maybe he'd give you a little wax figurine of a woman in a coffin or a book made out of his own skin or perhaps just something simple like a notebook full of criticisms."

I force a laugh. "No, he's just... I don't know. He took me to dinner, and he's been pulling out chairs and giving me these little touches—like brushing his hand over my arm when he likes a line I write. He's just touchy and stares at me with this really weird look..." The traffic light turns red, and I brake, staring out at the strip mall busy with people spending their money.

"Aw, EA's in love." She tosses her head back, laughing as she slams her palm on the dashboard. "Bless him."

Obviously this seems funny to her, but the more I replay the way his dead eyes will lock on me from across the room, the more my stomach knots. I panic a little. "Janine, I'm serious. There's something weird about him."

"Oh, there surely is."

"It makes me uncomfortable."

She glances at me, her smile fading. "He can do that. When I first started working with him, every once in a while, he'd give me the heebie-jeebies. He's just... difficult—complicated. Antisocial and awkward. But it's not like he'd ever force himself on you or anything. He's a good guy deep down inside. Just a bit of a weirdo, you know?"

"He ate raw deer meat today while staring at me."

A scowl forms on her face. "Yeah, well, that's just gross."

"I don't know if I can finish this book with him if I'm honest. I can't explain it. You'd just have to be there to understand how weird all this is." The light turns green, and I gently press down the accelerator.

She shakes her head. "You gotta finish it. Please, for the love of God and my sanity, finish this book with him. How far in are you guys?"

"About forty thousand."

"Okay, so what, two more weeks if you guys get after it? I'll come stay up there and snuggle you if I need to. I promise, honey, he's odd, but he's harmless. I've worked for him for five years. I mean, hell, I've cussed him out a time or two, and I'm still here."

My phone rings. Janine keeps talking as I dig around in my purse, attempting to keep my eyes on the road.

"Let's just go grab some food. I swear that cabin is enough to creep out Alfred Hitchcock, you know? Out in the middle of God's country and all those damn animal heads staring at you. And then throw in EA and his antics..."

"Sure."

She points out of the window. "Applebee's okay with you? They have the best raspberry cosmo—"

"Yeah, it's fine." I stop at another traffic light and grab my phone from my purse, staring at the number flashing on the screen. I press Ignore, but *she* calls right back.

"You can turn," Janine says.

I glance away from the phone and floor the gas, nearly fishtailing as I turn into the parking lot. There's a spot right to the side of the entrance. I pull in and put the car into park, my phone still ringing.

Janine glances from me to my phone and back at me. "You gonna answer it?"

"No." I hit Ignore again. And immediately, my mother is calling again.

Janine raises a brow. "Someone really wants to talk to you..." She opens the door and steps out of the car. "If you need a minute, I'll just be at the bar."

The door slams shut, and I watch Janine sashay to the front of the building. The phone vibrates again, Bush's "Comedown" playing from the small speaker. Listening to the song, to the beautiful lyrics, I stare at the number, wondering what the hell she wants. Mother's never been persistent with anything in her life, being a parent included.

My pulse picks up, that angry heat flooding my face when I press Answer and raise the phone to my ear. "What?" I can't control the hate in my voice. I really can't.

"Baby," she slurs, "I'm *so* proud of my baby."

"Excuse me?"

"Your writing." A hacking cough comes across the line. "Momma's so proud of you."

My skin crawls like I imagine it would if I were covered in a pile of writhing maggots. She must have heard about me getting that job with Edwin. *Fucking bitch.*

"I bet you are," I scoff.

"And what's that supposed to mean?"

"I guess now you want to try to be the supportive mother you should have always been, huh? If you think I will ever forget the shit you did to me, the shit you put me through—"

"I did the best I could," she says.

"Well, could've fooled me. Telling your daughter she's worthless and pathetic and will never amount to anything. Stupid. Ignorant..." I can still hear the disdain in her voice when she'd shout those words at me. "A mistake. A pain in your ass. That's the best you could do, *Mother*, really?"

"We all make mistakes. I am proud of you. I always knew you'd be something great. My little girl, a *New York Times* best seller..."

Closing my eyes, I shake my head in disbelief. She really thinks I'm going to hit a list with Edwin and give her something. "What are you fucked up on right now? Meth, crack, heroin, or are you just drunk?"

"I'm—"

"I don't care." I cut her off because I couldn't care less. "And I wouldn't go around bragging about what an accomplished daughter you have just yet, *Doris*." I want to squash any hope she has right now. I want to rip away any glimmer of happiness she may be experiencing from the thought that by giving birth to me, she has any right to a damned thing. "That little writing job's not working out so well. I'll probably quit it soon."

A raspy laugh crackles over the phone. "I should've known better. Should've known you were still that lazy piece of shit I raised. Giving up just when things are getting good." *And there she is, the woman who taught me about love and humanity. There she is.* "You're a disappointment. Ruined my damn life, and when you have a chance to make it a little better, you don't. Fifty dollars here and there don't do much. You did it on purpose, didn't you? You did this to piss me off—not giving to your poor mother. You'd let me die before you'd give me a damn thing worth a shit, huh, you—"

I hang up and block her number, something I should have done a long time ago. The sad thing is no matter how horrible some people are to you, sometimes all you want to do is prove to yourself you are worthy of their love—even when their love is worthless. And how fucked up is that?

Gripping the phone, I clench my jaw and fight back the tears. The thing is, I feel like a fool because I always had hoped that something would change. I thought maybe one day I could have some type of relationship with her. As much as I feign that it doesn't bother me, as many times as I've told people I don't care if she hates me, I do. Wanting love is just human. I just knew that I'd eventually do something to *deserve* her love, to prove to her I wasn't a mistake, but really, that's just pathetic. The only reason she would ever have a relationship with me is because I'd be able to give her something. And what kind of relationship can you have with a parasite?

I am a product of my environment through and through. And fuck her for that. The person who should have loved me unconditionally treated me like shit, and I know that's why I am untrusting and too often only see the bad in someone. I want to see all the ugly pieces of a person and make my mind up about how and why they will let me down—why I'll never be good enough for them. Because if I already know that I'll never mean anything to them, well, they can't hurt me, can they? Let someone get just close enough then push them away. Never believe a compliment, a promise. Hell, I hardly even believe myself half the time.

I close my eyes and shake the tears away because she's not worth it. I cry. She wins. I quit this job with Edwin. She fucking wins.

Moments.

There are moments in each person's life where everything shifts. Emotions morph. Hurt turns to rage. Love turns to hate. People change. It is the nature of life, for life is merely a metamorphosis.

I sit in Janine's car, watching the happy little families drift in and out of Applebee's, watching strangers carry out their lives like animals in a goddamn zoo. A woman in a too-tight black dress saunters in, some stupid man stumbling after her; she's most likely going to fuck him, and he'll never call her again.

Jax. I could fuck Jax, and I bet he'd never call me again.

Another couple stops at the car on the other side of me, kissing with the type of passion you usually only see in movies; in six months, she'll likely find him fucking her best friend.

Jax wouldn't do that.

A young man and woman stop by the curb, arguing. His face is red, and she's fighting back tears.

Jax wouldn't yell at me like that.

A mother scolds her child.

I would never do that.

An elderly man with an oxygen tank sits on the bench by the door and lights a cigarette.

He's saying "fuck you" to death.

A hoard of teenagers race out to their parked cars— BMWs and Mercedes.

They'll never know what it is to struggle, which means they'll never really appreciate a fucking thing.

And as I watch the shit show we refer to as life, I realize it's just one big ball of fucked-upness.

I climb out of the car, smiling at the old man puffing away on his cigarette as I reach for the door. He grins, and his entire face wrinkles. The entrance swings open, and the heat from inside sends a small buzz floating through my body.

"Welcome to Applebee's," the hostess mumbles, barely looking up from the stand, her unkempt hair falling in front of her eyes. "How many?"

"My friend's already in here," I say as I spot Janine tipping back a drink at the bar. I weave through the group of businessmen clogging the entrance, bumping into a few of them.

I'm almost to the bar when Janine sets her drink down and taps her red acrylic nail over the wooden countertop for the bartender. He glances in our direction.

"Another cosmo, my dear sir," she says.

A flirtatious smile crosses his face as he looks at me. "What'll it be, sweetheart?"

"A cosmo."

And he turns, reaching for the bottle of vodka behind him. I pull the chair out beside Janine, and she looks over at me.

She nods. "Uh-huh. Noticed this time you didn't say you don't drink." She laughs. "Told you that bastard'll drive you to the bottle."

The man places a napkin down, dumps a little salt on it, then places the martini glass in front of me, the dark red liquid threatening to spill over the edge.

I pick up the glass and chug it then place it on the counter. "I'll take another one. Extra shot, please."

The barkeep nods, and Janine whacks me on the back. "Attagirl."

For an hour, the conversation drifts back and forth from EA to Janine's string of ex-husbands, and I lose count of the drinks I've had. But my head is swimming, and my body is warm with this blissful fog of "I don't give a shit about anything." I kind of like this feeling. Maybe too much.

"And that's why I divorced husband number three," she says, arching a brow. Janine hops off the stool. "I'm going to the ladies' room. Order me one more, then we need to get a taxi or something because I definitely can't be weaving my way up that fucking mountain. And neither can you."

She stumbles off to the restroom. I dig my cell from my purse, but instead of calling a cab, I dial Jax's number, and now I have the phone pressed to my ear, my heart drumming into my throat with each ring. I debate hanging up and convincing myself he'll only hurt me. He'll be that guy who fucks me and leaves me, that guy who yells at me in the parking lot. Any of the bastards I sat and watched an hour ago.

But the second I hear his voice come over the line, instead of panicking and hanging up, instead of stumbling over my words, I say, "I want to see you."

He takes a moment, swallowing hard. "I've been waiting to hear you say that. McClintock's off South Street? Fifteen minutes?"

And... shit. "Uh, yep. Sounds good. Sure..."

"And there's that sure again," he says with a laugh. "Fifteen minutes it is then. Don't be late, or I'll arrest you."

"Yeah, um..." I fidget with the damp napkin beneath my drink. "Okay..." I don't know how to handle him. I want to laugh. I probably should laugh, but I suck at social cues. "I'll see you in a few."

I hang up and glance down at what I'm wearing in a complete panic. A Nirvana T-shirt, jeans, and Chuck Taylors. *Fucking amazing.*

I'm in such shock that I actually just initiated this that I barely notice Janine when she comes back. "Honey?" She grips my shoulder. "You okay? You look a little mortified."

"I, uh..." I glance up, swallowing as the panic really sets in. I grab my drink, down what little bit is left. "I just called Jax."

She beams as she motions for the bartender. "And?"

"I'm supposed to go meet him... shit, that's so rude. I'm sorry, Janine. I don't know what I was—"

"Oh, it's fine, sweetie. I'm just fine right here with my cosmos and..." She squints to read the name tag on the bartender's shirt. "Randall. Me and Randall will be just dandy, won't we?"

He ignores her and continues wiping down the counter.

"Where are you going?" she asks.

"McClintock's or something like that."

"Oh, that's just a block over." Her eyes widen, and she claps. "Talk about fate." She grins as she brings her glass to her lips and takes a sip. "Go on now. I've got my phone. If it gets too late, I'll take an Uber or"—a slight giggle bubbles from her lips—"go home with Randall."

Shaking my head, I grab my purse and head to the door, playing out a thousand scenarios of why I shouldn't go. I groan and push the door open, still in shock that I actually called him and agreed to meet him.

The entire ten-minute walk to the bar, I obsess over how I'll mess this meeting with him up. The thought of having to talk to him, having to come up with conversation, nearly paralyzes me. I'm bound to say something dumb or awkward or just... random. And then he'll give me some weird look, and I'll get all nervous that he's wishing he'd never met me, wishing I were some normal girl. A normal girl... a fucking normal girl...

The bar's dark and fairly empty. I walk straight to the counter and take a seat, crossing my legs and immediately picking at my nails.

"Want a drink?" the old man behind the counter asks.

I hesitate. My head's already dizzy from the drinks I had at Applebee's, and although it is tempting, I decide maybe since this foggy feeling is what incited that phone call in the first place, I shouldn't have another one just yet. God knows what I'd end up saying then.

"Oh, no thanks," I say, forcing a nervous smile.

He shoots a confused look in my direction, shrugs, then walks off to the other end of the counter to serve another customer.

And I wait. And wait. And wait.

"You sure you don't want a drink? You look like you could use one." The bartender laughs.

I glance at my watch. He's nearly fifteen minutes late. Which means he's probably not coming. "Uh... I'm—"

The bell over the door jingles, and I stop mid-sentence, turning around to find Jax walking toward the bar, his fingers running through his thick hair. Much to my dismay, my heart goes into a full-on sprint. I hate that a man can do this to me. I hate that I want him. I hate the vulnerability because it's an all too familiar feeling, dredging up things I'd rather not contemplate.

"Ah, just in time," he says with a smile as he pulls the bar stool out next to me. To my surprise, he comes in for a hug, placing his muscular arm around me.

What in the hell do I do? Hug him back or just... I awkwardly return his hug, and he kisses my cheek lightly.

"It's great to see you again. Sorry I'm late. My partner was being a pain in the ass," he says as he takes a seat.

"It's fine. And, yeah, it's good to see you too." I can't seem to calm my racing pulse, and soon enough, that fidgety nervousness overtakes me, so I flag down the bartender.

"Now, I may be wrong here, but are you *sure* it's good to see me?" He chuckles. "Seems like every time I see ya, you've got that little scowl on your face."

Ignoring his comment, I glare at him. "Do you want a drink?"

"No, I don't drink anymore," he says with a slight smirk. "I quit last night." As the bartender approaches, Jax nods toward the top shelf. "Give me a double Jameson, neat." He motions to me. "And whatever she's having."

"Yeah, exactly what I thought," I mumble as I turn my attention to the man behind the bar. "And I'll have tequila, straight. Thanks."

Jax shoots me an impressed look. "I like your style.

Sounds like we've had the same kind of week."

I toss my head back on a laugh. "Yeah, well, maybe. Who fucking knows?"

The second I glance at him, my nerves get the better of me. I don't know what the hell I'm doing here with him. This is only going to end in a disaster. *Shit*. Now he's smiling, and I damn near melt but manage to keep a straight face. I don't want him to know he has any kind of effect on me because that's when they know you're vulnerable.

"So anyway..." I clear my throat. "Sorry I just kinda called you. I just, I don't know." I shrug, my cheeks warming. "Needed to get out and, uh, yeah..."

The bartender places our drinks in front of us.

Jax immediately wraps his hand around his, tracing his finger over the glass. "Sweetheart, I'm working a case where, a few days ago, we pulled a girl in ten different pieces out of an abandoned house. Seeing your name pop up on my phone was the best thing to happen to me all day." He takes a long drink of his whiskey, his unfocused gaze straying toward the wall of liquor bottles, as if something is weighing heavily on his mind. "You use that number any time you want." He redirects his attention to me.

"Thanks." My leg is furiously bouncing. I bite my lip, struggling to come up with the appropriate thing to say. "And that sucks..."

"Sorry." He grins, taking another drink. "Probably a

little too much information for you. I'm just... I don't know. It's just been a hellacious week." He scratches at his beard, shaking his head slightly.

I grab my drink and tip it back. Swallow. Then turn the glass up again. The cheap tequila burns my throat on the way down, but shit, I can't drink this fast enough.

He eyes me with a grin, shaking his head. "Fuck, I've been known as a drinker in my day, but tequila... fuck that. Too many bad experiences with Señor Jose back in college."

"Yeah—" Another quick gulp. "I've not had any problems with it. Not yet at least." *But at this rate, tonight may be my first...*

"Well shit, there ought to be some sort of award for that."

"Oh, I'm sure there is..." And... here is that awkward silence. I stare at him, that dirty part of me wanting to undress him with my eyes. Imagine his heated, stifled breaths next to my ear as he has his way with me—

"You know, your conversation skills are quite impressive." He laughs.

"Oh, fuck you!" As soon as I say that, I cover my mouth with my hand. A Freudian slip he'll never pick up on, hopefully.

"Hey now, this is only our second date. I don't think propositioning me for sex is very ladylike." That damn grin again. "Do you?"

I bite my lip, hard, and narrow my gaze. My foot is

furiously shaking, making the small amount of tequila left in my glass slosh against the sides. *What would that girl do? What would she say?* "Trust me..." The alcohol is buzzing through me, making me not really care what comes out of my mouth. "That was *not* an offer." I laugh and tip the drink back again, smiling around the rim. *I can be that girl after all.*

He motions with his hand to catch the attention of the barkeep. "Bartender, another drink for the lady please." He shoots me a quick, mischievous glance. "And another one for me."

"If you're trying to get me drunk, too fucking late."

"I suppose that's why I heard from you tonight?"

"Maybe." I lightly touch his arm because that's what *that* girl would do.

"No EA to keep you company? Or, I guess, *Edwin* as you call him."

"Again, fuck you," I whisper. I lock my gaze with his. The second I realize my hand is rubbing his hard bicep, I jerk it away. "But, you know, if you'd rather me leave..." I go to stand, and he quickly places a hand on my shoulder.

"Hey now, you better sit that cute butt of yours back down." His hand lingers on my shoulder until I'm fully seated again.

His fingers drift down my arm before returning to his glass. Chill bumps sweep over my skin, and I find myself wishing he'd put his hand back on me. Touch me just a little longer.

My gaze falls from his eyes to his full lips, and all I can think about is kissing him. *Fuck, I hate this.* My hand quickly wraps around my glass, my eyes never leaving those lips of his as I suck back the last of my drink. "Fine. I'll stay... for a minute at least." Then I giggle. *Dear God. Who am I?*

"A minute? And how does a guy go about spending *more* than just a minute with you? Does he have to be an author? Because I'll tell you what, I can't write to save my life, but I'll put together the nicest picture book you've ever seen. Penguin cops or some shit like that."

Shaking my head, I nearly choke on my drink. "I'm sorry. Penguin cops?"

"I'm just saying that shit should be worth at least a couple hours."

"Wow," I say through laughs. "You're special, Jax."

"I'm glad you can see that so soon. Usually it takes a lot more convincing on my part. I prefer the term unique though."

"Okay." I arch both brows. "We'll go with unique."

The bartender places the next round of drinks in front of us, and I push mine aside.

Jax eyes me as if he's trying to figure me out, sizing me up. "I just can't read you, Miranda..." He tilts his head, his eyes narrowing.

"Cross."

"Miranda Cross." A deep smile fills his face. "And I'm a fucking cop. Do you know how bad that makes me look?"

"Look, don't feel bad. I've spent my entire life perfecting the art of being unreadable."

"Did you perfect that before or after the RBF?" he asks, a laugh ready to bust loose from his lips.

"Excuse me? I don't have resting bitch face."

"Now, now, it's a good quality to have. I bet more people on airplanes try to talk to me than you. And then there's the whole mall kiosk issue everyone else has to deal with. I bet they never ask *you* if you'd like to try pine-scented, age-defying lotion. That's a win if I ever saw it." A laugh finally does break through, and he shakes his head before taking down more of his whiskey.

I'm trying my damnedest to keep a straight face. "Okay, first of all, I don't fly. Second, no, they don't talk to me, but maybe it's because I don't need age-defying lotion yet, asshole."

"You don't fly? What, do you fucking teleport? And maybe that is what it is... because of course you don't. Ooor... maybe it's the fact that they think you want to kill them and eat their babies." He's smiling, those damn dimples popping.

I look away from him and stare at the bottles of liquor on the wall, my heart banging against my ribs as I trail my fingertip over the curve of my glass, wishing it was him I was touching, relishing... "I hate flying." I glance back at him.

"You know, it isn't plane victims we're zipping up into body bags every day." There's a soft smile on his face. "A lot more stuff to worry about in this world than flying, my dear."

"Yeah, I know. Just one of those things..." My eyes drift back down to his lips and pause for way too long. But I just want to kiss him. I shouldn't, but I do.

"Hey, we all have them. Don't even talk to me about fucking dolls. Those porcelain motherfuckers with the beady little eyes..." He shakes his head.

"Oh, I hate those things too. My mother had tons of those. Most were clowns." I shudder thinking about that collection.

"No fucking way." He laughs, his eyes wide. "My sister and I used to have a babysitter who had clown shit fucking everywhere. I'm talking wall-to-wall. Our parents weren't home very much, so I had to live with that shit for a while. I didn't sleep very well those days." He smiles, his eyes taking me in as they move from my lips to my eyes then back again.

I grab his arm before I realize I have. "Yeah, I had nightmares about them. And then Stephen King's *It*... ruined me. I'm convinced that was the moment I officially became fucked up."

"Holy shit, you have no idea. I've always been a big-time reader. Read that shit when we were visiting family in

Texas back in sixth grade." Lifting his brows, he gives me an understanding nod. "That shit changes a fucking kid. I'm talking scar-city type shit."

"'We all float down here...'" I shake my head. "Gutters. I avoid them at all costs."

"God, that's awesome." He laughs and raises his glass to me. "Well, here's to a mutual hatred of dolls and clowns."

Nodding, I clink my glass against his and laugh before setting the untouched drink back on the counter.

"So... I'm not very good at this kind of thing." He points at himself then at me. "Whatever this is. I actually haven't been out on a date in a long, long time."

"And you think I am? What with my *impeccable* conversations skills and all?" I laugh. "Yeah, I don't do people. Ever. But you..." I trail off before I say something I shouldn't.

"So if I'm brutally honest with you, you won't hold it against me?"

"Nah."

He gently grabs my arm, pulling me toward him. I have no choice but to follow his lead and grip the edge of the seat with my hands to keep from sliding off the stool. His other hand comes to rest on my cheek, his eyes intensely set on mine. When his thumb tenderly brushes over my jaw, my heart bangs against my chest, heating my body. I can't help but to lean into his touch. It feels too right. Too perfect. He inches forward until his lips meet

179

mine with such a soft touch I'm not even sure he's really kissing me. Within seconds, he takes my bottom lip into his mouth, his teeth nibbling just a little before releasing. He brushes his fingers into my hair as his lips crash hard against mine again. And from that simple touch, my entire body goes limp, every last inch of my skin heating. He cups the back of my neck to pull me closer and deepen the kiss. Just before I give in to him any further, I tear away, my heart in my throat as I stare at him.

A confused expression crosses Jax's face, and I immediately regret pulling away.

"Everything okay?" He looks around, but no one's paying us any more attention than we're paying them. "Sorry about the PDA... your lips are too distracting."

And now I feel like an idiot, so I do the only thing I can think to do—I grab him by the face and drag him to me, closing my eyes, and kiss him again. A subtle moan slips from my lips because, damn, his lips feel good like this. They're soft and warm and just... *right.*

And... this is bad. I know this is dangerous because I generally don't like people touching me, but Jax... there's something about him that I crave, possibly need—which means, in the end, I'm going to get hurt. Or maybe I'll just end up hurting him.

I go to move away, but this time, he grabs the back of my head, giving me one tender kiss before he releases me, his eyes locked on mine. And even I, with my lack of social understanding, can pick up, by that desperate glimmer in his eyes, that he feels the same way. And that's scary as shit.

Jax trails his rough fingers over my jaw, a soft smile settling on his face. My cheeks warm; my body flushes.

"Hmm," he says, settling back in his seat. "I could see this being a problem."

"What?" I feel a scowl form on my face, and he chuckles.

"This." He touches his finger to my lips. "Kissing you is kind of addictive. And I have quite the addictive personality."

I should probably say something instead of staring at him like an idiot, which is exactly what I'm doing right now. "You're ridiculous," I mumble.

Heat floods my body, and I turn in my chair to face the wall of liquor, my heart thumping in my throat. *Really? Ridiculous? That's the best you had? You could have said, "I like kissing you too. Thanks." Anything....*

Jax laughs, bringing his drink to his lips as he shakes his head. "Ridiculous, huh?" He smiles around the edge of the glass and winks.

I have no idea what I'm doing here, why I'm drawn to him like this, but I don't like it—and I like it all at the same time. Something about him seems safe and familiar, and as we sit here and talk, with every stupid, awkward comment I make, he grins. Maybe he gets my little quirks.

By the end of the night, I have my arm slung through

his as we walk to the exit. I find myself leaning closer to him, pulling in the scent of his cologne. I too easily get lost in his smile and those eyes that tell me there's so much more to him than most people try to see.

We round the corner of the brick building, turning into the dark alleyway that leads to the parking lot. We've barely made it two feet before Jax stops and gently pushes me against the rough brick, pinning my shoulders to the wall. We share an intense stare in the brief moment before his lips crush mine. His hand sweeps up my neck and cups the side of my face as his teeth rake over my bottom lip. He pauses, his warm lips barely resting against mine.

"Yeah, I'm definitely in trouble," he says with a sweet smile.

And in this moment, I know I'm fucked. Because even though I hate the vulnerability, the way he makes me feel is worth the possibility of having my heart ripped out. And if you know that's what will happen, are you really that vulnerable after all? So I give in to him.

I wrap my arms around his neck, tugging his body flush against mine. I try to quiet all the thoughts whirling around in my head so I can just enjoy how right this feels because it's not often I've felt anything in my life was right. But Jax, at this very moment, with his soft lips pressed against mine, his hands roaming over my body... that's exactly how he feels.

CHAPTER SEVENTEEN
Edwin

"Killing Time"—City & Colour

My fingers wind around the leather steering wheel, my breath fogging the driver's side window with each angry exhale. I knew it was a man she's been talking to. I could tell by the way she spoke, the way she reacted, the stupid, silly little smile on her face. But I didn't for a second think he'd be local. I didn't think that of all people fucking Janine would play a role in it. I could *fucking* kill her. My thoughts roam to Janine lying on her back with both hands pointlessly held up in defense as an ax comes heaving down on her. Splitting her fucking face in two after mangling her hands and fingers. The thought brings me immense pleasure, and a smile tugs at the corner of my mouth.

I *will* kill Janine.

For an hour, I've been sitting outside the bar, rage flooding my veins, adrenaline simmering just beneath the skin, ready to explode.

Watching them joke and laugh and kiss, seeing him

take what is rightfully mine right before my fucking eyes...
it takes everything in me not to remove the gun from my
glove box, walk into that fucking bar, and shoot every last
motherfucker in there. All I can think about is them going
to a motel room, his hands roaming over her body. I'm
overwhelmed by visions of him penetrating her and her
loving it. I bet she'd love every fucking minute of it.

Miranda doesn't think of me like I think of her. If she
did, she wouldn't be giving herself away like this. She
wouldn't be hurting me like this. The pain suffocating me is
overshadowed only by an incredible anger I don't think I've
ever felt. I slam my palm against the edge of the steering
wheel over and over until my entire hand stings.

I'm struck again with an intense urge to kill... anyone
and anything. Fuck plans. Fuck methodical thinking.
Someone's going to fucking die tonight, but it's gotta be
smart. I think of Janine as I put the vehicle in drive, but I
know her murder *must* be planned—if I ever hope to not be
caught, that is. She's just tied to me too closely.

A whore on Tenth Street will have to do. I tuck my hair
into a hat and pull it lower over my face. Just as I pull my
vehicle onto the road, a lifted truck, metal balls dangling
below the tailgate, comes screaming past me. I stomp on
the brakes just as the truck's horn blares and a skinny
middle finger darts out the window.

I feel a slanted, wicked smile fill my face as anger
surges through my body until I'm in an all-out tremble.

Streaks of light take up my vision. Rationale fades.

I pull my vehicle out slowly and follow the truck, which is now quite a ways down the road.

To my complete satisfaction, the truck continues out of the city and into the farm-rich countryside. I follow him for a good forty minutes, a safe distance behind, anticipation shaking me to my core. As a thick patch of darkness surrounds us, the city lights long since faded in the rearview, I snag a police light from my glove compartment and set it on the dash. I've never used it before, but right now, I'm happy I picked it up.

I flash the lights, and moments later, he pulls to the side of the barren road. I pull in behind him and put the Range Rover in park. Grabbing a Bowie hunting knife in its sheath in the glove compartment, along with a snub-nose revolver, I climb out of the vehicle. I slip the revolver into my front pocket and the knife behind my back in my waistband.

The walk is endless. Each step sends shivers up my spine. I can taste the kill. I can smell the iron in his blood. And I see Miranda's lover. In my head, it's him I'll be killing. It's his pathetic eyes staring back at me in horror as the life is ripped from him.

One day it will be.

"There a problem, officer?" the redneck asks, arching his head out the window just as a bullet rips through the door.

His high-pitched squeal lets me know I hit him, and I can't help but smile. A German shepherd barks at me from the backseat, its lips reared back, teeth gnashing, but he's leashed to the back door.

Opening the man's door, I direct the gun toward the dog's head. The man's confused eyes meet my own. I crook my neck and smile.

"Wh-why are you doing this?" he bellows, two hands grasping his blood-soaked knee.

I shift the revolver's aim from the dog, down to the man's already destroyed knee, and pull the trigger again. A blast ricochets out into the vast nothingness. The man slams his head back into the seat, screaming in pain. The dog wildly licks the man's face.

I crack a smile, studying his thrashing body as I stow the revolver back in my front pocket and retrieve the knife from my waistband. I hold it in front of his face, letting him get a good look at it.

He whimpers as he bats at the mess that once was his knee. "Please," he begs hoarsely. "Please, stop." His eyes drift to mine, pitiful as can be. "*Please*."

"Please, save me your tears. I have no use for them. Now your blood." I grin. "That's a *whole* other matter."

I pull the knife back then thrust it up into his chin. All six inches settle in his skull.

I catch a glint of moonlight off the sharpened blade through his open mouth, then with one quick motion, I pull the knife back out.

All I see are the whites of his eyes as he slouches over the middle console, motionless.

Slipping the blade back into its sheath and returning it to my waistband, my eyes wander to the dog in the backseat, still barking wildly and sending surges of anger throughout me. I want to kill it too, but before I can retrieve my revolver, a brilliant scenario plays out in my head—a dog eating its owner. I've read stories about it, and the idea fills me with a giddy, childlike wonder.

Depositing the revolver back in my pocket, I pull the knife out of my waistband as I turn the car off with my other gloved hand. Shutting his door, I creep around to the back passenger side door. I open it and quickly cut the leash before closing it again.

I wander back to my truck, a smile taking up my whole face as I imagine what it will be like for the man's family to walk up on this scene, the dog snout-deep in the man's guts. I imagine his family on the news, crying over their stupid little redneck fuck-up who was "going to make something of himself one day." *Please*.

As I reach my Range Rover, the police light still spinning blue and red into the quiet night, my eyes drift back to the metal balls hanging from the back of his truck... those stupid fucking metal balls. I *hate* those fucking things.

CHAPTER EIGHTEEN
Jackson

"My Name is Human"—Highly Suspect

"How long's it been here?" I ask as we pull the Charger up behind a mess of county police vehicles taking up the side of a two-lane country road outside the city.

The road is completely closed, with police tape surrounding a jacked up Ford F-150. A swarm of cops and medical personnel stand around, presumably bullshitting as they await our arrival.

"Farmer called it in around noon. He'd seen it sitting here all morning," Tommy says as he groans his way out of the passenger side.

I meet him at the shoulder of the road, and we both duck under the police tape. A sergeant—Sergeant Callahan, his name tag reads—meets us behind the truck.

"How y'all doing?" he asks, extending a hand.

I shake it, and Tommy follows suit.

"Just another day in the life. What do we got here?" I ask.

"Well, first off, you noticing anything odd about this little scenario?" The sergeant motions to the truck.

I scan it, see nothing out of the ordinary, and my eyes meet his again. He's got a knowing look in his eye and a smile tugging at his lips.

"Look closer." He smiles.

I look again, scanning the truck more intently, and I can tell Tommy catches it as I do because he bursts into a wild fit of laughter. The other officers around the scene look at him judgingly, shaking their heads, and after seeing what I've just seen, I can understand why.

A set of balls—a human set of balls—sack, pubes, veins, and all, is tied with rope to a pair of metal balls that hang just below the tow hitch.

I crouch to look at them, my hands rubbing my cheeks and my head shaking slowly.

"That's got to be the funniest shit I ever seen right there." Tommy snorts, continuing to laugh obnoxiously loudly.

"We've got a murder victim in that truck, Detective," the sergeant says sternly, pointing toward the truck.

Tommy tilts his head, a smirk on his face and an easy look in his eyes. "Sergeant, with all due respect, go ahead and fuck yourself. You need us. We don't need you. Remember that." Tommy takes one last look at the balls with a chuckle before he walks to the driver's side door hanging wide open. "Hoooo shit, partner. You're gonna wanna see this mess."

As I meet him by the open door, the smell of ammonia hits me hard and forces me back a few steps. "Holy fuck," is all I can manage.

"Yeah," Tommy responds. "Looks like somebody was trying to cover their tracks, huh?"

"You're not fucking kidding," I say, scanning the man slumped over in the driver's seat with his pants around his ankles and a patch of fatty tissue where his dick and balls should be. "You think he fucking used enough ammonia?"

"I think he wanted to be real damn sure." He nods toward a German shepherd lying limp beside its master's head, a gunshot wound to its stomach. "Think it had anything to do with the dog?"

"I think you're on to something."

CHAPTER NINETEEN
Edwin

"London Bridges"—Second Skin

Fuck. Fuck. *Fuck*. I pound the steering wheel as I speed down the country road to the nearest twenty-four-hour Walmart ten miles away, a bloody aftermath left in my wake.

I can't believe I could be so fucking stupid. Why did I go back? Why didn't I just leave it as it was?

As I steer with my knee, I wrap a dirty T-shirt from the backseat around my bleeding hand. That piece of shit dog bit me. My blood at the scene, my own fucking DNA, has the downfall of my entire career playing out in my head. If a trooper happens to be driving by, as unlikely as it is, and sees a truck abandoned on the side of the road, he's likely to check it out. When he discovers a mutilated body on the other side of the truck window, I imagine it's only a matter of time before they link it to me. My whole life spent as careful as can be, yet I wind up fucking myself in the end.

Walmart is only moments away though, and I pray

they have what I need. Whom I pray to, I'm not quite sure, but somebody better fucking listen.

As if a punchline to a *fucking* joke, a car jerks out from the side of an overpass onto the road behind me, and blue and red lights pierce my back window in flashes.

I toss the bloody T-shirt to the floor and kick it beneath my seat, digging the revolver from my pocket. I imagine killing the officer as he approaches then speeding back home. I'll take my briefcase with all the necessary escape material—fake passport, driver's license, cash, and disguises—and Miranda to the Asheville airport where my private plane sits waiting, ready to take me to South America forever.

Miranda and I will begin anew, killing and writing under a new name. My career—our career—will be reborn. She'll have to learn Spanish of course, but I can help her with that.

Instead, I slip the revolver into the middle console and slide my bleeding hand beneath my leg, readying my driver's license, insurance, and registration with the other.

A portly officer approaches, a flashlight shining into my open window. "Good evening. Any reason you're going so fast this evening?"

I hand over the documents and he takes them, analyzing each. I force a smile. "Just got caught up in a night drive, officer. I'm an author, and when I get writer's block, sometimes I just gotta get out and drive. Lose myself to the music, you know." I laugh as I scrutinize the officer.

His focus is still directed toward my driver's license. He finally looks at me with an eyebrow raised, a slow smile creeping over his lips.

"Lucky for you," he winks and disgust ripples throughout my body, "I've met my quota of tickets for the month." He hands me back my documents before rapping two knuckles against the car door. "You have a good night and slow down, alright?"

"Sure thing, officer."

Then he turns on his heel and heads back to the cruiser with a dance in his step. A wide smile takes up my face as I pull the Range Rover back onto the road, shaking my head at my own damn luck.

CHAPTER TWENTY
Miranda

"Take Her From You"—DEV

I watch a flock of geese fly over the top of the pine trees, losing myself for a moment. I glance back at the screen, my eyes drifting to the word count that's barely budged over the past day. Yesterday, Edwin refused to write and locked himself in his bedroom.

This morning, he sat down, wrote a disjointed paragraph, started swearing at the computer, chucked the keyboard across the room, then hopped up and went out to the shed. All morning he's been going back and forth from the cabin to the shed.

And now, he's just pacing, his cheeks red. Finally, he plops down on the sofa, turning the TV on, and flips channels. Stopping on the news, he groans and leans over his knees, dragging his bandaged hand through his messy hair. I glance at the time on the computer screen and breathe a sigh of relief. Janine should be here any minute, and she can't get here fast enough.

I pull up my email, reading over Jax's messages for the tenth time today:

I bet that pretty little voice of yours sounds even better when you beg.

I don't beg, was my reply.

You say that now, but wait until I get you all alone and naked, teasing you with my mouth. I will have you begging me to be inside you.

And I find myself smiling like an idiot. These emails started off innocently enough, but over the course of a few days, they've turned into foreplay. Message after message. Each one more descriptive and vulgar than the last. I skim over more of his promises—threats—and exhale.

I'll ruin you...

I'll let you.

I like it rough.

I like to be choked.

It's much easier for me, at least, to come across as flirtatious by using unspoken words, when I'm not face-to-face with someone who can hear the slight tremor in my voice, the uncertainty. I am, after all, a writer. It's been two days since I saw him, and no matter how hard I've tried, I can't get him out of my head. A distraction—Jax is a distraction. I try to plot or write, and somehow, my train of thought veers from screaming girls and hacksaws to his lips pressed against mine, his hands in my hair... me naked beneath him. *To me being* that *girl.*

The floorboards creak. The smile fades from my face as I turn in my chair to find Edwin looming behind me, his gaze glued to the computer screen, his nostrils flaring. I glance back at the message, close the screen, and clear my throat.

"Uh..." I push back from the desk and stand, skirting around Edwin, whose stare has yet to move away from the computer screen. "Janine should be here in a few. Sure you don't need anything from town?"

"No."

I swallow and give a quick nod as I grab my purse from the coffee table and head toward the door. It's cold as shit outside, but I don't want to be in here with him. "Okay, well—"

"When are you going to be back? We need to write."

Write? Now he wants to write. No, I think he just doesn't want me to leave. He wants me here with him.

I freeze, my hand on the doorknob, my hairs standing on end. "I don't know."

I breathe a sigh of relief when I pull the door open and see Janine's car already in driveway. When I turn to close the door, Edwin's crossing the living room, his jaw tensed, fists clenched at his sides. "Miranda..."

Janine's horn honks. She clambers out of the car, shielding her eyes. "I've got another splitting headache." She opens the passenger door and plops down into the seat.

"Annoying bitch," Edwin mumbles, catching the door and slinging it open. He shoves past me and stops on the steps.

Janine rolls down her window, and I quickly walk past Edwin. I swear I can feel his eyes boring a hole into the back of my head as I hurry down the stairs, nearly missing the bottom step and tripping. I catch myself and go straight to the car, opening the door and climbing in without giving Edwin another glance.

"Oh"—Janine arches both brows and nods toward the porch—"he looks pissed."

I don't look back. I don't want to.

"Janine," he shouts from the porch.

"Yes, dear?"

"I need to meet with you." His voice is shaking, and I imagine that if I were to look at him, he'd be talking through gritted teeth. "Soon," he says with a growl.

"Anything you want, EA." She waves and smiles before we pull off. "He's such an asshat," she says with a laugh. "No wonder he doesn't have a woman. What woman is gonna put up with a moody bastard like him?"

I shake my head and stare out of the window, lost in my thoughts as I wind down the mountain.

Janine glances at me with a raised eyebrow. "So, drinks first? Don't you stand me up."

"Trust me, I need a stiff one. A really stiff one. You're a saint for dealing with him for as long as you have."

Nodding, she smiles. "Drinks to get you relaxed and your inhibitions lowered before you're off to that beautiful specimen's house to be manhandled like a two-dollar hooker."

"Dear Lord."

"And I do want the gritty details, hun. My pussy's starved." She cackles, slapping her knee.

———

The chilly breeze sweeps across the patio, cigarette butts and napkins tumbling over the concrete pavers. I shiver and pull my jacket tight across my chest.

"Now, this is classy. Two ladies out on the patio for a midday glass of wine." She holds up her glass and winks at me. "Classy."

"Yep. Winos have always been the top-notch of alcoholics."

She covers her mouth to keep from spitting out her wine, choking at the same time as she laughs. "Well, who knew? Little Miranda Cross *does* have a sense of humor after all—a dry sense, but a sense nonetheless."

"Sometimes." I lift my glass to my lips and take a steady sip, the bitter white wine sending another chill through my already cold body. "I should have had coffee."

"And Baileys? Oh, oh, or Jameson. Irish whiskey in coffee is phenomenal."

"Or just coffee." I eye Janine. She's always drinking. And while she manages to keep it together, at the root of it all, she is, in fact, a drunk.

"Nope. You need alcohol." She smirks before raising her glass once again. "Because you need to live a little. Remember what I said about experiences?"

"Yeah, yeah..."

The waitress brings a mother and her little girl out onto the patio and sets menus in front of them.

Janine glances at them, her lip curling ever so slightly. "Kids. Yuck."

"What?"

"They're like little parasites. They suck you dry and leave you for dead—and with a bunch of nasty stretch marks." She glances at me. "Anyway, you need to fuck him. Just to say you did it. Don't expect anything from it except maybe a good orgasm."

"Janine..."

Her eyes remain fixed on mine, one brow arching, one corner of her lips curling up into a devious grin. "Men like that... that's all they are good for, hun. Trust me on this one. If you let them get their grubby little claws in too deep, they'll just break your heart." She nods. "Fuck him. And leave him."

"Fuck him and leave him?"

"Yep. Be *that* girl. Fuck him hard and fast and good. Be the one he'll never be able to get out of his mind. The one he always wonders what the hell happened to."

I stare off, not at anything exactly, just a random patio

paver. *That* girl. She would fuck him and leave him.

"Mommy..." The little girl at the other table is attempting to whisper, but she's only talking in a rather hushed voice. "That lady. Look at her."

"Shhh."

I turn just in time to see the mother scolding the little girl, her eyes briefly flicking up to mine before she looks away.

"Rude little demons, see." Janine adjusts her shirt, tugging the neckline down enough to showcase her impressive cleavage. "Marilyn Monroe, she said something along those lines," she says, pushing back from the table and grabbing her purse as she stands.

"Said what? That kids are rude little demons?" I down my wine so fast a momentary wave of nausea settles over me.

"No, that 'a wise girl kisses but doesn't love, listens but doesn't believe, and leaves before she is left.' Something to that effect." She smiles. "And Marilyn was *that* kind of girl."

"Who had an affair with a president and died before she was thirty..."

Janine's already to the gate, one foot on the sidewalk. "Exactly. She experienced life, hun. All you've done is write about it."

CHAPTER TWENTY ONE

Miranda

"Strange Love" - Halsey

I stand on the porch, staring at the doorbell, my nerves completely rattled. I go to ring the bell but stop, quickly digging through my purse for a tube of lipstick. I touch up my lips, comb my fingers through my hair, and take a deep breath. *Ring it, Miranda. Just do it.*

And I do, my finger shaking. For a split second, I debate turning around and leaving. Because what am I going to do once I step through that door? It's six in the evening. And I'm at his house. Why? Because he thinks he's going to fuck me? That is what that email basically said. And here I am, because I want him to fuck me... *shit...*

The lock clicks. My pulse speeds up. The knob twists. I take another deep breath. The door opens, and here I stand, my mouth hanging open with not one fucking word to be found.

"Hello, gorgeous," he says, a beer in one hand, a tired look in his eye, but a smile still on his face. "I'm glad my emails didn't scare you off too much." He sidesteps and puts a hand out for me to come in.

"Nope. Not at all." I step inside.

He closes the door, sighing. "It's been a hell of a day. It's nice to see a friendly face."

He leads me to a couch in the front living room. The inside of his house is bare except for the artwork he most likely found at a garage sale. No photographs or personal touches. Only essential furniture and an old box TV.

"Can I grab you something to drink? I've got beer or some whiskey or vodka."

"Sure..."

"Well, I can't really pour 'sure' over ice, so what'll it be?" he asks with a snarky smile.

"Vodka's fine. Thanks." I settle back into the couch, watching as he makes his way into the kitchen adjacent to the living room.

He opens the freezer and pulls out a bottle of vodka. "So how's working with EA going?" With a grin, he drops ice into a glass, fills it with vodka and water, and walks it carefully over to me. He hands me the drink before retrieving his beer from the coffee table and taking a seat beside me. Really close beside me.

"Uh, okay, I guess..." I bring the glass to my lips and take a slow swig.

He sips his beer and reaches for the TV remote, flipping through a few channels before turning to me with a hopeful look in his eye. "Speaking of... when do I get to meet this guy?"

"Yeah..." I laugh and shake my head. "Trust me, you're better off not meeting him. It'll ruin the image you have, I assure you. The more time I spend with him, the more certain I am that he is actually a psychopath."

He laughs loudly, shaking his head, and sets the remote back down. "Yeah, I'm sure he is. I'm sure Stephen King has seen his fair share of dead bodies too. You gotta be a little fucked up to write that kinda stuff. I mean, aren't you?" He winks, his lips spreading into a smile—and those damn dimples...

At first I'm put off, offended. But he must be joking. So I pretend to be *that* girl. "Yep." I smile. "Sure am, and *you* invited me into your house." My eyes drop to his full lips, and I inch just a little closer to him. "And *now* you're all alone with me."

"Lady, I've spent four years on the streets of Asheville and three more before that killing towelheads. If anybody in this room is bordering on psychopath, it's me." He lets out a nervous laugh, and his hand comes to rest on my thigh. He lifts the beer bottle to his lips but doesn't take a drink. "Shit." He chuckles, his thumb gently gliding over my leg. "You must think I'm nuts. I'm totally kidding by the way."

Shrugging, I take another drink of vodka, trying to not pay so much attention to his hand on me. "Sure you are."

"Oh, I only mean it wasn't any of that stuff that knocked my screws loose. That came looong before."

"I'm not worried. At least, if you plan to kill me, make it quick. I wouldn't be much fun anyway. I'm not the begging type..." I immediately bite my lip and shove the drink back in my face.

He slants an eyebrow, a mischievous smirk on his face as he removes his hand from my leg. "Begging, you say? Now, there's a thought..." He taps a forefinger against his chin.

I give him a good shove in the arm. "Don't even think about it."

"Hey," he says, nudging me back, "you brought it up. I'm a man. I can't help where my mind runs from there."

I glare at him, my heart slamming against my ribs because I want him to make me beg. I want to fuck him. I shouldn't, but I do.

"Oh, and I have handcuffs," he says with a laugh, pulling back as if bracing for another hit.

"Are you really supposed to use those off duty? Wouldn't that be abusing your authority or something along those lines, *Detective*?"

"Well, Ms. Cross, who exactly is going to know other than us?" He looks around then back at me. "I won't tell if you don't." He winks and clicks his tongue.

Heat floods my cheeks, my chest, every last inch of my body. I'd let him handcuff me and choke me. I'd let him do a number of things to me I wouldn't let any other man do because he looks capable. He looks as though he would ruin me. And that dirty part of the soul that every last one of us has, it wants to be tainted. It yearns for something to make me feel filthy.

A smirk inches across his face, and he grabs my jaw, his eyes dropping to my lips as he leans in. His mouth is warm and soft and right against mine. His tongue parts my lips. His fingers work into my hair. And the next thing I know... he's dragged me into his lap. I'm straddling him, slowly grinding my hips against his and moaning into his mouth like a whore. Like a dirty, filthy whore. And all that does is make him kiss me harder, more deeply, more brutally. His teeth rake over mine, his hands now on my waist, his fingers skimming underneath my shirt.

"Fuck, I want you," he says against my lips, and I nearly lose all control. *He wants me...*

He grabs the waist of my jeans, pops the button, and rips the zipper down. And just like that, his hand is between my legs, his thick finger rubbing over my clit, across me, sliding into me. It's been so fucking long since I've been with a man—never a man like him—and I find myself holding my breath, my head tossed back. His lips work over my neck, every few inches biting and nipping at me. His knuckles press against me, bruising me as he fucks me with his hand.

All I want to do is touch him. Timidly, I trail my hand

over his shirt, his hard chest and stomach evident beneath the thin material. I hesitate when I get to the waist of his jeans. I take a moment to feel his fingers inside me, flexing and bending. I swallow, my chest rising in ragged swells as I slip my hand inside his jeans, the head of his dick already wet from pre-cum. My fingers slide over him, my body drowning in a heat of want and need and primitive desire. And just as I pull his fly open, just as I wrap my fingers around the girth of his dick, just as I feel my muscles clenching, my body submitting to his touch... doubt slams over me.

I push away from him, stumbling as I stand and back away from the couch, out of breath. "I, uh... I, um..." I swallow. I feel my cheeks heat. My gaze strays from his dick to his hand wet with me to his shocked expression. "I..."

"Do you not..." His brow furrows. "I mean, I thought..."

"I just, um. Give me a minute."

I turn and hurry down the hall to the bathroom, closing the door behind me. I stare at myself in the mirror. Red lipstick is smeared all over my face, my chest splotchy. I'm going to fuck him, and he'll leave me, and then I'll hate him, and I think the biggest problem is I don't want to hate him. I want to pretend there is something good in this life. Pure and like those goddamn romance novels I so despise because at the end of the day, the idea of love weakens even the most cynical of creatures. The thought of owning someone the way that emotion does... it's addictive. And if I fuck him, that stupid fucking fairy tale will be incinerated.

Fuck the fairy tale. This is real life, Miranda. Fuck him and leave him. Use him just like you were used by all those people. That man—I need to look at him as an experience. A muse. Because love is bullshit. People are selfish. And that feeling of having a man inside you, having a man need you so badly, even if it is only for a few moments, well, I guess it's better to have that than nothing at all.

I call his name, staring at my reflection and telling myself not to regret this. "Jax, will you come here for a minute?"

I hear his footfalls come down the hallway. They stop outside of the door. He pushes it open, one brow arching when he peeks around the door. I motion him in with a curved finger, a slight smirk on my lips.

The second he steps in, I grab his face and kiss him. Hard. My palm glides over the front of his jeans, his swelling dick evident. I grab it and bite his lip. And then hands are on my shoulders, slamming me against the wall. Jax covers my mouth with a brutal kiss. His fingers dig into the curve of my waist, and a low growl slips from him. His teeth rake over my bottom lip, and he presses his body against mine, pushing me hard against the wall as he grabs the bottom of my shirt, bunching the material up. His rough hands drift up to my neck, his fingers slowly wrapping around my throat just below my jaw, the kiss growing deeper, rougher with each passing second.

I grab his arms, my fingers grasping his hard biceps for dear life. I want him to fuck me to within an inch of my life. To the brink of death. And this slow teasing is winding me up like a tight coil, the tension nearly unbearable.

One of his hands drifts down my stomach, his fingers skimming the waist of my jeans before he grabs between my thighs, palming me. I can't resist this urge to push against him, ever so slightly grinding against his hand. I should fight this, drag it out, but his warm lips, the taste of his tongue, the way it feels as if he's everywhere on my body but not nearly enough, not in the way I *need* him to be—I'm close to losing every bit of fucking control I have. His hands find their way into my hair, and he fists it, yanking my head to the side as he tilts his head ever so slightly, his eyes locked on mine in a stare so intense I fear I may lose a piece of myself I'll never get back if I give in to him. And you know what? He can fucking have it.

"Fuck, Miranda," he breathes before his lips meet the crook of my neck, his teeth sinking into my skin just enough to force a hiss from my mouth.

"Goddammit, fuck me already," I say in a breathy moan, a plea, my fingers grasping for the bottom of his shirt and tearing it over his head.

And with that, clothes are ripped off, hands are all over the place, feeling, touching, gripping. His naked body presses me into the wall, the heat of his skin driving me completely mad. He fists his cock, and I open my legs, giving myself to him. His mouth is on my throat, each uneven, ragged breath rushing over my skin. Each groan right at my ear. He rubs the tip—the warm, hard tip—against me.

"Shit, you're fucking wet," he says right before he grabs my ass, forcing my hips against his. The head barely goes in. He moves away from the wall, dragging me with him, his fingers digging into my ass as he lifts me and sets me on the edge of the sink. "I'm going to fuck you right here."

I grab my knees, opening my thighs as I pull my legs to my chest. He looks at me spread out just for him, for him to do whatever the fuck he desires. That look—that is what every woman wants. The way he's looking at me is completely unhinged, out of control. Like an animal, a beast.

There is no foreplay, no warning, no soft caresses. Jax slams into me so hard I have to grab the sink edge to keep from falling into the bowl. I gasp just like a whore. I moan. I pant. And at moments, I hiss because he is fucking me hard. Using me. Skin slapping against skin. And to be honest, I've never felt more like a woman than I do with him buried so deep inside me it hurts, his hands gripping my hips with such strength I know I'll be bruised.

His hands move up my sides, trailing up my back until

he's cupping the back of my head. He presses his sweaty forehead against mine, his gaze boring into mine as he fucks me. And I'm losing it. I want to scream. And I do.

"Fuck. Fuck. Fuck!" My hands slip over the counter, knocking most everything—cologne, toothbrushes, bottles—into the sink. "Oh God. Oh fuck. Oh fuck." I'm about to fall over that edge into an oblivion of moans.

"Oh, no, hun. Not yet you don't." He drags me off the sink and turns me around, bending me over the counter. "I want you to watch me fuck you." He stares at my reflection with a slight smirk. He grabs my hair, wraps it around his wrist, and yanks my head back as he leans down by my ear. "I wanna watch you come, Miranda."

He thrusts back inside me, and I watch him tear into me. Jaw clenched, head thrown back—until I can't keep my eyes open any longer, until my vision starts to swim. My chin drops to my chest.

"I said *watch* me," he says in a growl, his hands wrapping around my throat and forcing my head up. He squeezes, and I moan. His fingers twitch over my throat, and I gasp. "You like that?"

I want to nod. To say yes. But I can't. I reach out to grab onto whatever I can. The tumbler on the counter is knocked to the floor, glass shattering all over the tile. Heat drowns me, buzzing over every last inch of my flesh, and my body goes limp within his hold. Weightless. In a fog of bliss and filth. Seconds later, Jax releases me, pulling out, grabbing his dick, and staggering back. I look up, watching him in the mirror as he tosses his head against the wall. His eyes close; his mouth hangs open, hard breaths coated with primitive groans rumbling from his chest as he comes on my back.

As soon as his orgasm has worn off, he glances up, his eyes locking with mine in the mirror. "Fuck."

I smile, pretending I am *that* girl who will just walk away from *that* guy. But I'm not. I'm really not.

CHAPTER TWENTY TWO
Edwin

"Down with the Sickness"—Disturbed

I can feel myself unraveling one strip of sanity at a time. What once I thought was normal, owed to me, now makes no sense anymore. My head is spinning, rage tearing through me like a drug. And it's all because of her, because I allowed myself to feel something for someone else for the first time in my life. *And how the hell could I let this happen?* I'm stronger than this... or so I thought.

It's all moot at this point. I'm bloodthirsty, blood-starved despite my kill on the side of the road. With the potential of being caught looming and the only woman I've ever loved ripping the charcoal heart out of my chest, I don't give two measly fucks anymore. Let me die a murderous legend. I guarantee my books sell ten times better than they already have. When they know that the murders were real and they can quietly live in sick fascination of my work, hiding their true selves from everyone, I will live on forever.

Before any of that happens though... I'm going to kill everyone. Starting with Chastity, then Janine, then I'll play with Miranda and her lover just a little bit. I'll make them fuck for me. Not with his dick though—that'll have been long cut off, seared with a blowtorch to stop the bleeding. No, he'll fuck her with a loaded gun—maybe a machete. The one thing that is certain, as certain as the setting sun, is that they will pay, and they will feel my wrath.

Chastity climbs quickly into my car, shutting the door and eyeing the interior. "A Range Rover. Nice!" She slips a hand on my leg, and I nudge it away. Her gaze falls on me, a confused expression on her face. "Everything okay, Taylor?"

"My name's actually not Taylor," I say, my eyes still on the road. "It's EA Mercer." I wait for reaction but get none.

"It's not surprising. A lot of people go by different names." She slips her hand onto my knee again, and once more, I brush it away. "Seriously, what the fuck?"

Her bitchy tone makes me want to slam her head into the dashboard until it's painted with brain matter.

"Fuck is exactly right. That's all I want tonight."

She looks around, finally realizing we aren't going to our usual motel. "Where are we headed?"

"To my house," I say, pulling the Range Rover onto the highway. "So the name EA Mercer doesn't ring a bell, huh?" I look at her, my eyes narrow, and she subtly backs away, a confused look on her face.

"Should it?" she asks, looking once more at the passing pines and moonlit road signs.

"It figures it wouldn't. People like you, Chastity, can't appreciate the art of the written word. God didn't gift you with that ability." I eye her up and down, my lip curled in disgust as if she had the plague. "He didn't gift you with much other than good looks and a tight pussy." I scoff and direct my attention back to the road. "And let me tell you, sweetheart, both of those fade, and as a fucking worthless street whore, I'm assuming they're going to fade real fast for you."

She backs up all the way to the door. "I want out of this fucking car right fucking now!"

"You're not *fucking* going anywhere." I shoot her a glare. "This is your destiny, sweetheart."

She starts to tremble, slamming her hand against the unlock button, but nothing happens.

A smile spreads across my face. "You think I'm that stupid? Childproof locks, my dear. Or slut-proof in this case."

Pulling a fist back, she thrusts it toward me just as I pull a cattle prod from my side door compartment and hit her in the stomach with it. Her body thrashes, eyes rolling, then she slams against the dashboard. Her body is limp, her eyes still open and staring right at me.

"Night, night, dear," I whisper, brushing her hair behind her ear before I turn my attention back to the dark, winding country road.

CHAPTER TWENTY THREE

Miranda

"Eyes on Fire"—Blue Foundation

I startle awake, and chills sweep up my spine. I'm still sore between my legs from Jax fucking me the other night, and I shift uncomfortably as my eyes adjust to the dark. But the second they do, I jump and scream.

Edwin's at the foot of the bed, one hand on the footboard, his dark eyes locked on me. "Didn't mean to startle you." A smile flickers over his face. "But we need to write. The inspiration's just hit, and it's..." A soft laugh bubbles from his lips. "Well, it's the most inspired I've found myself in such a long time."

There's a long moment of silence—maybe minutes—because the one thing I've grown certain of over the past day is that Edwin is not stable. And while I don't want to be near him, it's probably in my best interest to appease him in any way I can.

"Uh, yeah, okay." I toss off the covers and plant my feet on the cold hardwood floor. "Sure..."

His smile deepens before he turns and opens the door. Wiping the sleep from my eyes, I stumble into the hallway after him with my stomach in knots. Edwin goes straight to the desk and turns on the lamp, then he pulls out my chair for me.

"After you, my dear." He brushes his cold hand over my shoulders as I take my seat, and my skin prickles.

I turn the computer on and wait for the program to boot up. The entire time, I feel him staring at me. I swallow before turning to face him.

"You are beautiful, Miranda."

"Thanks," I whisper as I direct my attention back to the computer screen.

"Beautiful *little* Miranda..." A short, ominous laugh rumbles from his chest, sending my heart into a panicked sprint. The program pops up on the screen, and Edwin begins to type. "Now, pay close attention."

She has no idea the ways in which the universe has lined up. No idea what a trivial piece of the puzzle she actually is. And that is exactly the way I want it. I want her to wonder whether I intend to kill her or whether I want to keep her. Forever. And ever and ever....

The typing stops. I can't force myself to look at him because I can literally feel him staring at me, so I keep my eyes trained on the screen. On that flashing cursor. On the word "ever."

"Dear Miranda... tsk, tsk, tsk, what ever shall I do with

you?" The legs of his chair scrape over the floor, and I cringe. "Water?" he asks as he makes his way through the living room toward the kitchen.

"Uh, yeah." I clear my throat and make a conscious effort to keep my voice from shaking. "That'd be great."

I watch as he rounds the corner, and the very moment he disappears, I open my email and type Jax's contact into the recipient line.

Please come get me. Edwin's scaring me.

I press Send, but the email remains on the screen, the cursor now turned into that little blue circle that keeps cycling around. I hear the door to the fridge shut. Footsteps. My heart is in my throat, pounding so hard my vision pulses. *Come on. Come on.* I attempt to close the browser, but the entire screen is frozen.

"I think we're at the climax of the story and we can—" He stops mid-sentence.

I close my eyes, wanting to burst into tears because I know he's seen the email message that is still centered on the screen.

"Well." He places a bottle of water in front of me. He doesn't say another word, simply turns around and crosses the room. He stops at the front door, pulls a key from his pocket. It's now that I notice there's an exterior lock on the *inside* of the door, and a knot forms in the pit of my stomach. Edwin locks the door. "You just don't understand, Miranda Cross. You really don't."

And with that, he disappears down the hall.

CHAPTER TWENTY FOUR
Jackson

"R&R"—The Classic Crime

Leave it to me to find the type of woman who's going to sneak out on *me* in the middle of the night. I've sent a few texts over the last two days, an email too... still nothing. I try to tell myself not to relentlessly check my phone and inbox, but it's a losing battle.

It couldn't have been the sex. I'm talented at very few things in this life beyond police and military work, but sex is definitely one of them.

I read her breathing patterns, her facial expressions, how her toes curled. I made sure to get it just right. Slow when I needed to go slow, when she was just about there, hard and fast to take her the rest of the way. I'm all about satisfying the women I'm with. Seeing them come and puddle into the mattress in a state of complete euphoria is everything. Them getting off gets me off.

So no, I won't even entertain that thought. My best guess is that she just played me like a dude. Fucked me and left me. Back to writing. Back to EA.

He's a legend, beyond rich, and considering she only spent one night with me, I guess he's a better lover too.

The email on the screen, which I've read at least twenty times, makes it perfectly clear I was played, and I was played hard. But at least I can say I got EA Mercer's girl. That's something. I read it one more time for good measure, a masochist to say the least. I revel in the pain.

I don't know who the fuck you are, and to be perfectly frank, I don't give a fuck. You need to stay away from Miranda. She's mine. I've seen the emails between you two. I know she's been seeing you. How does my dick taste by the way?

It stops now.

No more phone calls, no more emails, no more fucking visits. She's getting her own fair share of shit for her transgressions, but I'll tell you, you will get much worse if you come near her again. I will fucking destroy you. Do you know who the fuck I am? Do you know the power I hold?

STAY THE FUCK AWAY FROM HER...

EA Mercer

NYT & USA Today Best-selling Author

www.eamercerbooks.com

"What the hell, man? You going home or what?" Tommy asks, startling me as he appears in my office doorway.

I shake off the email. Removing my glasses, I rub a finger and thumb in my eyes. "Eventually. I'm dog tired. Just wanna go over this last case a little more." I motion to the file in front of me.

"What are you thinking?" he asks, taking a few steps in and slipping on his coat.

"Oh, nothing in particular. Just working on the why. Why him? Why there? What did this guy do to get his balls hacked off?" I ask.

"Ex-wife, maybe. Current wife who caught him cheating?"

"That's what I was thinking too, but his wife's been dead for three years. No girlfriend. And then there's the whole DNA thing," I say, shaking my head and exhaling a heavy breath.

"Garcia said we should have the match for that second blood type any time now."

"Another reason why I'm still hanging around here. We've got that match. We've got our killer."

"Well, fuck, man, the dude's still gonna be dead tomorrow." He shrugs and smiles. "Go home and get some damn sleep."

I roll my eyes, putting my glasses back on. "Have a good night, Tommy."

He gives me a two-finger salute, makes a quick turn, and exits the office. Something I should be doing too, but I can't. Not just yet.

I pick up the case file from my desk to go over it one more time, but as I do, I hear the ding of a new email come from the computer. Thinking of Miranda, my eyes dart up and catch the notification just before it vanishes.

Miranda Cross.

I click the icon, and the email comes up. I have to read it a few times to be clear of what I'm seeing.

Please come get me. Edwin's scaring me.

My mind races over all the things that that could mean, none of them good. Maybe that's why she hasn't contacted me.

I stand from my chair, stuffing the file in my briefcase then grabbing my leather jacket from the coat hanger, and I make my way out to my truck as quickly as I can.

———

I'm fifteen minutes out, the thick forest making the night even darker. The moon is the only thing illuminating the small country road ahead of me. My nerves are stirring a sick feeling in my stomach, and I'm wishing I had at least brought Tommy with me. Something just doesn't feel right.

My cell phone ringing from the center console pulls my attention. The screen reads, *Asheville Police Department.*

"Hello?"

Nothing.

"Hello?" I repeat, louder this time.

I hear a faint voice come over the line, but it's too quiet to make out. I put the phone on speaker, lifting it high and watching the signal bars bounce between one and two.

"Hey, you'll have to speak up. I've got shit service," I call toward the raised phone, an eye still on the road in front of me.

"Peralta. Can you hear me?" Detective Garcia's voice comes over the line, still fuzzy and distorted.

"*Yes*. Yes. Tell me you've got some good news for me."

"Oh, I... something for... all right. You sitting down?" he asks. "You're gonna wanna be... this."

"Fuck, man, I can barely make out what you're saying. Just fucking spill it already."

"...second blood sample... from the truck came back... match. And you'll never believe who... is," he says, cutting in and out. He says something else, but it's too distorted to make out.

"Garcia, you there?" I ask.

"I'm here."

"Who is it, Garcia? *Tell me.*"

"Well, you know that author you're so fond of..." he says before the line cuts off completely.

Goose bumps race up my arms and legs. My mouth gapes, and the blood drains from my face as I process what I've just heard. *It couldn't be. It must be a mistake.*

But then my thoughts stray to Miranda's email, her words sending my imagination into a tailspin of blood and carnage. *Please come get me. Edwin's scaring me.*

I dial 9-1-1 and thrust my foot against the accelerator, racing along the narrow country road and hoping to God I'm not too late.

CHAPTER TWENTY FIVE
Miranda

"Big Bad Wolf"—In This Moment

My palms are slick with sweat. Adrenaline buzzes through me, and my pulse drums in my ears. I glance at the bay windows that don't open, my heart sinking into the very pit of my stomach. *He's going to kill you.*

I jump up from the desk, my chair falling to the floor with a loud bang. I take off down the hall and run into my bedroom. Edwin comes storming from his room just as I slam my door closed and lock it, pressing my back against it as I attempt to catch my breath. The door shakes behind me.

"Miranda..." he says in a low growl. The door handle jiggles.

My eyes lock on the window and I run to it then throw the curtains back. A small gasp leaves my lips when my gaze lands on the lock. I quickly turn it and try to push the old window up, but it doesn't budge. "Fuck!"

"Miranda." There's a loud thud behind the door. "I

told you that when you find the person you love, you can't ever let them slip away, dear." Another wham against the door. "And—" He grunts with another whack at the door, this time wood splitting. The curved blade of a hatchet smashes through the door just before Edwin's fist comes slamming through.

I scream, tears pouring down my cheeks as I push against the damn window. "Fucking move. Open, goddammit."

I use all of my weight and the window barely lifts, the sill creaking as I glance over my shoulder. I watch his fingers grab at the lock and twist it. The door flies open and slams against the wall.

Edwin's face is splotchy-red, his eyes wide when his broad frame steps over the threshold and into the room.

"Please..." I turn and place my back against the wall as I scoot in the opposite direction of him. "Please, Edwin... I..."

"So you do beg," he says with a laugh.

He steps toward me and I clamber across the bed, nearly tripping when I jump to the floor. I just make it to the doorway, my fingers gripping the busted frame in an attempt to get into the hallway more quickly, but his hand grips my shoulder, yanking me back into the room. I trip and fall. My knees bang against the hard floor, pain splintering down my shins.

"Please," I whisper, knowing how cliché and pathetic

it sounds, but when you're at the mercy of another person, it's the only word you can find.

Edwin fists my hair and violently drags me to my feet with a groan. "I really hate to be like this with you. Really I do." He shoves me by the back of the head into the hallway. "Walk. Don't hesitate."

I'm in full on sobs when we reach the front door, and he places the key in the lock. The latch clicks, and that sound echoes in my mind, my knees threatening to buckle. The door swings open, slamming against the wall as the cold night air wraps around me, making my already tense muscles grow more rigid. Edwin pushes for me to walk down the steps, his fingers digging into my shoulder as he turns me toward that fucking shed.

The wind picks up. The waning moon illuminates the heavy gray storm clouds, making them pop against the black sky. Twigs snap underneath my bare feet. Pebbles and rocks cut into my heels. A low groan of thunder rumbles through the sky just as a few cold drops of rain hit my arms.

"You know, Miranda, I thought you'd have figured this out by now, but sometimes, well, sometimes I guess fate doesn't slap both people in the face hard enough, huh?"

"What are you talking about?" I ask.

He comes to an abrupt halt, and his already unbearably hard grip on my hair tightens, my scalp burning as several strands are ripped loose. My knees go weak, and

STEVIE J. COLE & BT URRUELA

I nearly collapse. Maybe I would have had he not had such a hold on my hair. Edwin tugs my hair and brings my face within centimeters of his. For a few terrifying seconds, all he does is stare at me, into me, through me. Part of me fears that, in this moment, he's taken a piece of me, that he's ripped a part of my humanity from me with that look alone.

"You and I, we are one. We belong together. My words should be yours and yours mine. Fate put you here for me." He inches even closer, his lips now resting against mine. "The sooner you see that..."

His words are lost when he presses his mouth against mine. I attempt to pull my lips in tight, to resist him, but he twists and knots my hair. The second I go to scream, he kisses me harder, slipping his tongue inside my mouth.

Before I can react to that, he's backed away, a wicked smile tugging at the corner of his lips. "See?"

And what do you do in a situation such as this? I try to think of a way to escape, but the thing is, I've read every one of the man's books. Every last sick and twisted word. I know how his mind works, and sadly, I know there is no way out. There never is. In every book—there is never an escape.

He keeps one hand tight in my hair as he pushes a key into the padlock hung from the door of the shed. The latch opens, and the lock falls to the ground before he opens the door and shoves me inside the pitch-black shed.

He releases me as I hear a moan from inside. A scream. The door slams. A lock clicks.

I have to cover my nose and mouth, fighting back the urge to vomit from the putrid smell of urine and feces and— I gag again, that awful smell actually coating the back of my throat as I drag in a breath. I bend over my knees, my eyes watering. This smell—*this* smell—is copper and sewage, rotting cabbage and flesh.

"No use in trying to get out. There's no one around for miles. I'd catch you before you got far," Edwin says, and I swear I can hear a smile.

A soft sobbing fills the room. I hear a slow *drip, drip, drip.* I don't want to know what that noise is coming from. I don't. My hairs stand on end, my stomach churning as my legs give out, and I fall to my knees, my head hung to my chest. And after only a second, I drop onto my hands, my palms landing in something cold and wet. I close my eyes. *Dear God.* I'm afraid to move my hands.

There's a soft buzzing sound, and an overhead fluorescent flickers on. I keep my eyes trained on the floor for I feel that may be the safest place for them, but nowhere in here is safe. The floor is covered with bloody boot prints. Underneath my hand is a mass of yellowed, congealed fat. That dripping sound that has yet to cease—it's coming from the blood trickling off the table right in front of me.

I want to scream. I attempt to scream. However, nothing but a rush of air leaves my lungs.

"Stop crying, whore."

I watch his boots cross the room and stop at the end

STEVIE J. COLE & BT URRUELA

of the metal table. Her cries grow louder, more desperate and helpless and godawful until they are full-on screams.

"Chastity," Edwin says with such a sense of calm it makes chill bumps scatter across my skin. "There's someone I'd like you to meet... Miranda?" A moment of quiet. "Miranda?"

Slowly, I lift my head and stare at him, my jaw trembling from the utter fear pummeling through my veins at this very moment. My eyes land on Edwin, one hand on that table and a soft—dare I say genuine—smile on his face.

"Stand up, dear."

I do as he requests, although my legs protest as I rise to my feet.

"Come here." Crooking his pointer finger, he motions me toward him.

It's not until I'm halfway across the room that I find the origin of the overwhelming stench that hangs like a thick, moist fog in here. Crumpled in the corner of the shed is a body. Decomposing and rotten. A sludgey mess oozes out from underneath the corpse. An axe rests in the middle of the head. The split is deep, the skull exposed, brain matter hanging from the open, disintegrating flap of skin above her ear. Dried blood and goop covers the entire torso, and gnats buzz around the corpse.

My body shakes, and my stomach muscles bunch and tense as my body repeatedly threatens to expel the contents of my stomach. I divert my stare to the floor once again,

231

back to the boot prints and fat and skin.

I can hear the girl on the table breathing. Her breath is hard and labored—staggered and riddled with sobs. Her toes come into my line of vision. Her ankles are cuffed to the table. Dark bruises cover her shins and the top of her feet. I swallow and lift my gaze to Edwin, purposely avoiding the rest of this girl.

"Miranda, this"—he motions toward the table as he arches a single brow—"look..."

My gaze falls to the table, and I stifle a cry. The blonde lies completely nude and bound to that metal table, just like the girl in our book. Her breasts have Xs cut across them. Burn marks cover her stomach. Small crisscross patterns are slashed over her thighs, her lip busted, her eyes purple and swollen. I tell myself this isn't real—just a bad dream. A story in a book. This is fiction because surely this is not my life right now.

"This is Chastity." Edwin trails a finger over the shredded skin of her breast, flicking the loose flesh.

She cries. I shudder. He grins.

"I've been saving her for years. I wasn't quite sure what for, but when I realized what you and I were meant to be, I knew why she was put into my life. Fate." He steps away from the table. "Fate, Miranda Cross. Just as you were meant for me, she was meant for us." He holds his hand out as though he expects I'll take it, but all I do is stare at him. A slight smirk plays on his lips. "Don't be difficult."

"I—"

He reaches behind him and pulls out a chair. "Have a seat." I shake my head, and within seconds, his bruising grip has latched onto my arms. "I said—have a"—he slings me down into the chair, and it tips back onto the hind legs before falling forward—"seat. You see, Miranda, details. It's all in the details, wouldn't you agree?"

"Edwin, I—"

He's grabbed rope from a rack beside the table. All it takes are three short strides for him to be right behind me, the rope wrapping around my waist and chest as he binds me tightly to the chair. He scoots the chair next to the table Chastity is laid out on before pulling his Macbook from a drawer built into the table.

"As I was saying..." He plops the laptop over a puddle of blood in front of me. The splat sound makes that pit in my stomach feel like a lead weight. "Details. I've always prided myself on vivid descriptions. The *accurate* descriptions of death and dying. No matter how good of an imagination you have"—he chuckles—"nothing short of experience can justly recreate it."

This man is mad. Insane. And I'm locked in this shed, tied to this chair with him and her and that poor dead woman in the corner. Rain pummels over the roof of the shed. The muffled sound of thunder barely rattles the walls, and from the way the ground just shook beneath my feet, that noise should have been much louder. Screaming will do me no good—just as his victims in the books are told. Screaming will do no good. There's no one for miles.

"Edwin." I swallow, fighting the urge to allow my gaze to fall to Chastity. "Please, don't do this."

He cups my jaw, his thumb rubbing over my cheek. "It's what must be done. You'll see how beautiful this will be. How perfect we will be together. How wonderful our words are. And when they read them…" A pleased smile interrupts his speech. "They will read our words. *Our* words. They will read our words."

Edwin checks my restraints before he boots up the laptop. While he waits, he drags a satchel from beside the table and lays out tools: a knife, an ice pick, a hammer, a lighter, and… a hacksaw. He runs his fingers over the jagged teeth, his eyes locking with mine.

Shaking my head, I glance at the computer screen. He jabs over the keys. The writing program opens, and he scrolls to the end of the document then shoves the computer back in front of me. "Write."

"Write?" I stare at the keys. "Write what?"

"My every move. Every cry and sound she makes." He picks up the knife and holds it over her face, his attention now directed at her. "As much as I enjoyed that mouth of yours on me…"

He places the blade inside the corner of her mouth, slowly slicing from it to the middle of her cheek. Her legs pull against the restraints. She screams—fuck, does she scream—her back bowing from the metal table only to slam back down.

He leans over her, his face inches from hers. "Shhh." He takes the knife and tears through the other side of her mouth and cheek, his eyes glued to hers. "I don't hear you writing..."

"I... I..." I shake my head as I stare at the keys, my heart banging against my ribs with such force I fear it may stop at any moment.

When Edwin slams his fist on the table, the handle of the knife clanging against the surface, I jump and Chastity wails. "Fucking write."

The knife rips through her fair skin, ruby blood weeping from the cut and mixing with her tears...

Edwin peers over my shoulder and nods. He points a bloody finger at the words on the screen. "Worthless. Say 'her worthless tears.'"

I type in the word, and he pats me on the back, making me cringe.

One thousand thirty-four words later, Chastity is barely able to keep her eyes open. They flit and flutter. She moans. Every once in a while, her fingers twitch. And I'm in tears, sobbing as my fingers shake over the keyboard.

Edwin uses the back of his hand to wipe away the sweat beaded on his brow, blood smearing across his forehead in the process. "I want us to do this last bit together. We'll write it together once we're finished." He reaches for me, and I jerk away. "Come now, Miranda."

He picks up the blood-stained knife, slips it underneath the rope, and quickly cuts it loose. Just as I go to stand, he grabs me by the throat, his fingers digging in so hard I can't manage to drag in a decent breath. He lifts me, my jaw pressing hard against his hand. I can't help the desperate gurgle that comes from my throat nor the way I'm clawing at his hands.

"Don't make me kill you." He releases me, takes the hacksaw from where he left it in her thigh, and hands it to me. "Take it."

I back away with a small step.

"Take it." He shakes it at me, a piece of mangled flesh falling to the floor.

Another quick, short step backward.

"Where do you think you're going to go, huh?" His eyes narrow, his gaze flicking to the locked door. "There's no way out."

And there goes my heart. Racing. Jumping. Skipping beat after beat as a dizzy heat washes over me. Edwin grabs my arm and drags me back to the table. He squeezes my wrist. His jaw tightens as he pries my fist, finger by finger, open. He takes my hand and wraps my grip around the slick handle of the hacksaw, covering my tiny hand with his huge one. I fight him when he attempts to move the saw over her throat, but after a few shakes and jerks, his other arm wraps around my throat in a chokehold. Eventually the blade is right above her throat.

"I'll help you," he whispers, nuzzling his nose against the crook of my neck. "Don't worry. The bone makes a damn terrible noise, and the spine"—he kisses right below my ear—"it's a bitch to sever sometimes, but we'll do it together."

I go limp, and the second that blade touches her skin, the first sensation I get—those vibrations of the saw tearing into her flesh and bone—I scream and shout and cry out to a god I never believed in.

What hell have I been delivered to? My eyes veer to the screen of the computer, to those wicked little words I've typed, and I know it's too late. My soul has been taken, and there is no way back from this.

CHAPTER TWENTY SIX
Jackson

"Limousine"—Brand New

The cold rain comes down in sheets over the windshield. The headlights of my patrol car bounce over the trees and the side of the cabin. I turn in to the driveway, not bothering to cut the engine when I jump out of the car, flashlight in hand.

Drawing my gun, I hurry up the steps to find the door wide open, all the lights on inside.

"Detective Peralta," I shout as I step inside the house. It's silent except for the ticking sound from the grandfather clock at the far side of the room. "Miranda?"

Silence.

I make my way down the hall, freezing when I come to the last room on the left. The door hangs from the hinges. The window is slightly cracked, and I walk over to it, shaking my head. Just before I turn to leave the room, I notice the shed on the back of the property.

Hurrying back outside, I round the side of the house,

my boots splashing in the mud, the cold rain soaking through my clothes. I aim the flashlight at the shed, the light reflecting off the droplets pouring down. On the ground in front of the door is a padlock. I reach for the door and raise my gun. The second it cracks, blood-curdling screams filter out into the night. I take a breath as I nudge the door the rest of the way open, shock rippling through my body.

Miranda glances back at me, her eyes riddled with fear, a hacksaw clutched in her hand and hovering over a dismembered bloody mess of a body. Blood is splattered all over her porcelain skin, her clothes.

"Make him stop! Make him stop, Jax," she cries.

I drop my gun to my side and stagger back a few steps before I grab onto the doorframe to steady myself. My eyes flit around the room in a desperate attempt to make sense of this all.

"Make him stop!" she shouts again, her voice strained.

Taking a step inside, I slowly lift the gun once more. Another steady step inside, the smell of death and blood making even my trained nose sick. "Miranda, put the saw down."

"He won't let me. Edwin, please," she begs. "Please let me go."

"Miranda..."

She shakes her head, covering her mouth with a blood-covered hand.

I aim the gun.

"Shoot him."

I swallow, my pulse hammering through my temples. "You're alone, Miranda."

Her eyes widen, her gaze veering to her left. "He's right there, Jax. Shoot him."

She looks so certain. So sure that it makes me question myself momentarily. I glance to her left, but there's no one there. "Miranda..." The gun is now shaking in my hands.

I glance at the corpse on the table, two large Xs cut across her breasts. My stomach sinks. Bile rises in my throat.

When I met Miranda, I knew there was some common thread, some connection, but I thought it was fate. *She shares my burden too.* I'd thought that but had no way of understanding just how fucking true and sick that commonality was. I had been hunting for the person who killed my sister, and all along, it was Miranda.

Fighting the urge to cry, my nostrils flaring, I raise my gun, staring down the sights into those hazel eyes I thought maybe, just fucking maybe, I'd found myself in. I close my eyes, the sound of her moans echoing in my head, the way she felt pinned beneath me searing through my skin. I swallow. I open my eyes.

"Jax... please. Help me." Her voice is barely above a whisper, fear in her eyes.

My throat goes tight. I shake my head. My finger

twitches over the trigger and...

CHAPTER TWENTY SEVEN
Miranda

"Paint It Black"- Ciara

Three months later

I stare at the white cinder block walls, humming "Singin' in The Rain." I can't get that damn song out of my head for some reason. There's nothing in here aside from the rickety cot I'm sitting on. No windows. No sheets. No pens. Nothing. Four walls and a damn cot.

"I know it's difficult to understand," Dr. Roberts says.

My gaze veers back to her, and she offers a sympathetic smile. I hate when she does that. I'm not fucking crazy. They all think I am, but I'm not.

"Detective Peralta said when he found you in the shed, you—"

"Fuck him," I say, gritting my teeth. I stare at the wall, my heart thumping against my ribs. "I hate him."

And I do. I still haven't figured this all out. To be

honest, it's about to drive me mad. *Actually* mad. Edwin is real, and no one will listen to me. But I've realized that Edwin must have used Jax to set me up—blame me for his murder spree. And I'd thought Jax wanted me. I'd believed him when he told me I was beautiful. Tears blur my vision, and I rock back and forth on the cot, trying to loosen the damn jacket. I close my eyes, and all I can see is Jax—that face, that smile, those dimples. I can feel his warm lips on mine, and my chest tightens at that bittersweet memory because I know everything he said and did was a fucking lie.

Shaking my head, I try to push away the thought of how he sounded when he came. "Jax told you I was insane. That I killed those girls. Did Jax tell you he fucked me? Just like a dirty little slut. He fucked me and used me."

Anger ripples through my veins, my skin heating, my temples throbbing as I recall the way he felt buried deep inside me, his hands on my hips. Just the thought of him makes me want to scream. I struggle against the fucking jacket, thrashing from side to side.

"Elizabeth—" Dr. Roberts reaches for that little red button, and I freeze. If she pushes that button, the attending will rush in and jab me with a nice sedative. I don't want that.

"I'm not crazy. I bet Edwin paid Jax to set me up. You know Jax saw Edwin. He arrested me and left Edwin there with those bodies. He'll see," I say, a subtle laugh slipping from my lips. "Edwin will kill him too. Watch."

And I hope he does. The thought actually makes me quite giddy, because Jax is a bastard. He made me believe there was some decency to humanity, that maybe I could be loved by someone. Love is bullshit. Everything about it is an ugly lie. Edwin was right—sex and money are all men are after.

"Let me know when he kills him, will you?" I smile.

"Elizabeth—"

"My name's Miranda." I clench my jaw. "Miranda Cross."

She inhales, tapping her pen over the edge of her clipboard before she glances at the clock. "No, your name is Elizabeth Ann Mercer."

I shake my head adamantly, fighting against the tight restraint of the fucking jacket they insist I stay in. "No. It's not."

"Yes. You are EA Mercer, *New York Times* best-selling crime author."

"No. That's Edwin." How he did this, how he managed to set me up like this, I still haven't figured out. But I can't really be surprised. He's a genius.

"Elizabeth—"

"I'm not answering to that. Miranda. I'll answer to Miranda."

She casts a stern look in my direction before jotting something on her notepad.

"If I'm not Miranda Cross, explain to me how I worked at the Little Novel Bookstore off Fifth and Main in Atlanta. How I was enrolled in Emory."

"You were never enrolled in Emory. You attended UNC. And that bookstore only exists in your books, Ms. Mercer."

"No, I remember. And James. Creepy James..."

"All in your novels."

I stare blankly at her. How can she be so stupid? Those places are real. I've been there. I've held those books. A brief memory flashes through my mind...I'm at my desk— no, at Edwin's desk—a steaming cup of coffee next to me as I type in the name "Little Novel Bookstore." I see the text pop up on the screen. I feel pride when I type the description of freckle-faced James. I *did* know a freckle-faced James...

I shake that thought from my head. "Just ask Janine. She'll clear all of this up."

Dr. Roberts arches a brow. "I can't ask Janine, Elizabeth."

"Well, why not? She'll tell you how crazy he is. She's the one who handpicked my manuscript to give to the bastard. She—"

"Janine's dead."

I fight the tears building in my eyes. Poor Janine.

"According to the decomposition of her body, she's been dead for months."

"That's not possible," I whisper.

A sharp twinge shoots through my head, and I close my eyes. For a fleeting moment, I remember the look of horror in Janine's eyes when that ax came down on her face. I can hear her screaming and wailing. But I push that thought away. It's not true. It's not.

"It's not true…" I mumble.

Dr. Roberts leans over her knees and takes a deep breath. "Elizabeth?"

I don't like her calling me that.

"Elizabeth, why did you keep her in that shed? All the others you discarded, but Janine… you kept her."

"I… uh…" Sweat builds beneath the collar of my jacket. I can feel it seeping from the pores above my upper lip. "I…"

Another memory of Janine flashes through my head. Her purple-and-black bloated body is slumped over in the corner of that shed, and I'm pacing the floor, talking to her. Yelling at her about my shitty reviews. No—that is a *mirage* because that cannot be a memory. Surely…

Dr. Roberts leans down to pick up a manila folder from the floor. She sifts through documents before pulling out a bundle of papers bound together. Exhaling, she flips through the pages, folds several back, then shoves the manuscript in front of my face, her finger hovering over a highlighted paragraph. My eyes scan the text.

It's late evening, and I'm alone at work. The best thing about this bookstore—the Little Novel Bookstore *off*

Fifth and Main—is it's hidden away in a crappy part of town. Hardly anyone ever comes in here. There's only a single small window at the front, and once the sun goes down, the store becomes dim and gloomy, the perfect place for me to lose myself in my books. No people and a nice little reading retreat—well, it's the perfect place to work, isn't it?

The bell over the front door dings, prompting me to bookmark my spot in Mercer's The Dark Deceit. It's the fourth time I've read it, and it still makes my heart race as much as it did the first time. I peer over the cramped shelves. I see no one, but I hear the soles of their shoes padding over the tile floor.

I nervously clear my throat, pushing a bit higher on my tiptoes. My heart slams against my ribs as I frantically glance around to see who walked in and why they're hiding. I have a habit of letting my imagination get the better of me, as I'm told most writers do—

I glance up from the paper. My stomach kinks and knots, bubbling with anxiety. "Where did you get that?"

"It was on your laptop. The one that was in the shed with you when Detective Peralta found you."

I swallow hard and close my eyes. This cannot be true.

"From the files saved, it looks like it was around August when you started your novel featuring Miranda Cross, a creative writing student from Emory, and a male author-turned-serial-killer, a *fictional* man you named

Edwin Allen Mercer."

"No." I shake my head. "He killed prostitutes. He fucked them... I couldn't possibly..."

"Exactly. And how did you know that?"

My jaw hangs open as I fumble for a logical answer. Because there must be one. "I... well, I-I mean. I mean..."

Another barrage of images floods my mind. Chastity on the bed, facedown and bound. Me behind her, pulling her hair and fucking her like I was a man. The image skips like an old movie reel, and I see myself in the diner, that greasy, nasty diner, and I am *alone*, the men across the counter staring and whispering because I'm talking to myself, the night we went to dinner—only one plate of food was delivered because he wasn't real. *He wasn't real....*

"But it's not the..."

Dr. Roberts takes a deep breath. "Elizabeth, you really have no recollection of these things? Of all the people you killed in that shed? The shed you built specifically to kill in? What do you think we should..."

Her voice fades into the background, just an annoying hum of noise within my cluttered mind. Did I kill all those people? Did I imagine all those things? Can I be that insane yet feel so sane?

I hear the latch of the door behind me open, then I feel fingers brush across my shoulders, my skin prickling.

"She doesn't understand, Miranda," Edwin whispers, his warm breath blowing across my neck.

I glance up at him, my pulse hammering in my temples and sending a jolt of adrenaline throughout my body. Slowly, I look back at Dr. Roberts, wondering if she notices him.

"What?" she asks. "What is it?"

I turn to face Edwin again, and he holds his finger over his lips. "Don't tell her. We have to finish the book first. It's almost done, but"—he nods toward Dr. Roberts, who is busy making notes—"she's in the way. She'd never let us finish it, my dear Miranda. And they must read our words." A devious smile crosses his lips. "They must read all of our wicked little words."

But I smile even deeper than he does because I know a secret—they *did* just finish reading. Every. Last. Fucking. Sentence.

NIGHT NIGHT, DEAR.

"Fiction is the truth inside the lie." –Stephen King

UPCOMING
Releases

WHITE PAWN - Coming January 16th, 2017

US: http://amzn.to/2e7iDAV

UK: http://amzn.to/2e8St2X

CA: http://amzn.to/2eltogy

AU: http://amzn.to/2eliCv2

At first you may think this is a story about love, well, it's not. It's not at all. It could have been. It had the potential to be, but he fucked all that up. I loved him. I loved him to the point of hate. With that said, maybe this is a love story of sorts, because surely to be obsessed with someone there must be a love story somewhere within the madness.

I haven't always been crazy...I swear. It's all his fault. Everything bad in my life is because of him. Justin fucking Wild...

QUESTIONS
for Discussion

1. Now that you have finished Wicked Little Words, how do you think the character's interactions, or lack thereof, tied into the ending?

2. What role do you think Jax played in the unraveling of "Miranda's" mental status?

3. Whose story do you believe you actually read? Miranda and Edwin's? Elizabeth's?

4. How did the ending make you feel? What impact did the last sentence have on you as a reader?

5. Now that you've read the story, do you recall certain things occurring throughout the story that make more sense now?

6. Did you find any similarities between Edwin and Miranda?

7. How do you think Jax feels at the end of the book? How do you think what he discovered about Miranda will affect him?

8. Do you think there is any redemption for "Miranda" in Jax's eyes?

9. Do you think it is possible for the imagination to muddle reality and fiction until a person is no longer certain what their reality is?

10. Do you think EA Mercer's success drove the author insane, or do you think it was something much deeper than that?

ACKNOWLEDGEMENTS
Stevie

There are many people who have helped with this book, but a special thanks goes to Heather Roberts for all of her hard work in promoting and helping keep me on track. You are a wonderful friend and publicist, and must have the patience of a saint to deal with me.

Thank you Joy Editing for the wonderful editing and proofreading job done by Cassie and Devon. And thank you, Leigh Stone for the beautiful formatting job (and for being an amazing person all around).

I'd like to thank Cara Gadero, Lucy Taylor, and Jen Lum for being such wonderful people and always offering support and advice. Love you ladies!

Taylor, it's been amazing writing this book with you. You're a talented writer and a wonderful friend.

Thank you to LP Lovell for being an amazing friend who will always be there when I have a mental breakdown. I know I have found a rare friend in you, my British Boo.

Stephanie T., I love you more than you could ever know. You have always encouraged me. I can't thank you enough for loving me the way you do.

AJ, I couldn't think of a better person to be my sea turtle.

Panda 1: I love you and our bamboo forest.

Angela, you make my heart smile.

Finally, to all the amazing bloggers and readers who support these books, thank you from the bottom of my heart. Without you, there would be no reason to write these words. Thank you for letting me do what I love.

ACKNOWLEDGEMENTS

I have to first thank the Lord. It's been a long road, and one I've veered off of frequently, but His love and guidance has never wavered. I will never forget the second chance at life He gave me.

Major David Gladney Taylor, thank you for being you and for the sacrifice you and your family have made for this country. You are in my thoughts always.

Michelle, Jake, Joanne, Joe, and Kay, thank you so much for accepting me into your incredible family. I feel honored and blessed to know you. It means the world that through such a tragedy, I was at least able to meet some of the kindest, strongest, most generous people I've ever met. Love y'all!

Pops, Brad and Britto, you are my strength. I know, without a doubt, I wouldn't be where I am today if it weren't for your love and support. I love you guys more than anything and can't thank you enough for sticking it out with me.

To my boys (and girl!), Rob, Krotch, Andrew, and

Beth, thank you for always having my back. You know I've got yours forever. Same goes for my VETSports crew, Kevin, Margaret, Jennifer, Jenifer, Johnson, Randy and Bryan.

Stevie, what can I say? You're an amazing co-author and an even better friend. This has been a wonderful writing experience and I look forward to many more.

To my book family, Golden, Michael, Harper, Heidi, Christopher, Reggie, Shauna, Mikey, Amy and of course the other R&E Frat bros, Michael, Daryl, SD, Seth and Eddie, y'all are amazing! This beautiful industry has been like a second family to me and it's because of you all. Thanks for all that you do, and more importantly, all that you give to others.

To Cat and Cara, thank you for all your hard work and for taking on the complicated job of keeping me in line! You two have been game changers. It's a true pleasure to work with you and an honor to have you on my team. I of course can't forget the other 3Bs who work tirelessly to get the right words out of me. Your dedication and commitment is unmatched and so very appreciated! Thank you Jen, Holly, Jenn, Lucy, Amy, Nikki, Blue, Stefani, Angela, Jennifer, and Kristen!

Last, but most certainly not least, a massive thank you to my readers. I never thought people would be interested in reading my stories. I never thought my words were worthy of sharing. You've instilled in me a total belief in myself and God's plan for me that I never had before. Without you, I'd be lost. You mean so much to me and I'll spend the rest of my life declaring it loudly. THANK YOU, THANK YOU, THANK YOU!

CPSIA information can be obtained
at www.ICGtesting.com
Printed in the USA
LVOW08s1251190117
521521LV00002B/246/P

9 781539 670537